FRIENDS
OF ACPL

j
High,
Maizie

MAIZIE

MAIZIE

Linda Oatman High

Holiday House/New York

Copyright © 1995 by Linda Oatman High
ALL RIGHTS RESERVED
Printed in the United States of America
FIRST EDITION

Library of Congress Cataloging-in-Publication Data
High, Linda Oatman.
Maizie / Linda Oatman High. — 1st ed.
p. cm.
Summary: Living with her father and sister in a trailer on
Welsh Mountain, twelve-year-old Maizie comes to terms with her
mother's decision to leave the family four years ago.
ISBN 0-8234-1161-3
[1. Mothers and daughters—Fiction. 2. Sisters—Fiction.
3. Single-parent family—Fiction. 4. Mountain life—Fiction.]
I. Title.
PZ7.H543968Mai   1995   94-22370   CIP   AC
[Fic]—dc20

To John, who gave to me a rainbow of faith, love, and patience higher than the Welsh Mountain and helped me hold on to my wish, never allowing it to fly away. And to our children: Justin, J.D., Zachary, and Kala.

A mountain of heartfelt gratitude is due to:

Stephanie Tessler, who believed in Maizie and in me.
Kent Brown, who gave me Stephanie.
The Highlights Foundation, which gave me the 1993 John Crane Memorial Scholarship and Chautauqua.
Margery Cuyler and Ashley Mason, who gave Maizie a home at Holiday House.
Thank you all.

Contents

Contents

MAIZIE

CHAPTER 1

The Wish Books

It was half past dark on a Saturday night and we were cutting mothers from the Sears catalog for our Mama Wish Book. Grace wanted a fancy Mama in a frilly dress, but the mothers I chose were from the Sporting Goods department. A dark-haired lady skimming across the ice in white skates was my favorite. She was smiling and looked as if she could give good hugs.

The Mama Wish Book was a yellow notebook left over from second grade, when I learned to write in cursive. I chose yellow because it's the color of hope. Grace and I had been hoping for a mama for a long time, and I suspect that Pa was hoping, too. He didn't admit it, though. Pa just buried his feelings somewhere deep inside his gut, like most of the men on this Pennsylvania mountain.

Our mama took off with the Rainbow vacuum cleaner man when Grace was ten months old. I would rock Grace to sleep at night and rinse out her diapers in the toilet, imagining Mama and the Rainbow man white-water rafting down the wild Youghiogheny River and laughing their heads off because Pa, Grace, and I were stuck on the Welsh Mountain like bumps on a log. Mama and the Rainbow man lived in an apartment near Pittsburgh, where jobs are plentiful and money grows on trees.

I was only eight when Mama left, four years ago. All I remember is that she smelled like lilacs, she had light red hair like mine, and her laugh sounded like shattering glass. Pa always said that she had the oddest sense of humor he'd ever seen in a woman. She must have been something. She named me Maizie and my sister Grace so that our names together would sound like "Amazing Grace." And Mama never even went to church, except for weddings and funerals.

I started the Mama Wish Book the day she left, by gluing her high school graduation picture on the first page of my cursive notebook. Even though the picture was black and white and wrinkled, I could see that Mama's eyes were twinkling. I used to pretend that Grace was the twinkle in Mama's right eye and I was the one in her left. Pa was her smile.

Four years later, the Mama Wish Book had 130 mothers. Most of them were from the Sears catalog, which seemed to have the best selection. Some of the pictures were crooked, as Grace insisted on doing her own cutting and pasting.

We also had a Baby Brother Wish Book. We always worked on the Mama Book first, because everybody knows that you must have a mama before there's any chance of having a baby brother.

Our Baby Brother Wish Book was a lot of fun because we included things for the baby,

like cribs with teddy-bear bumper pads and
walkers and rattles and rocking horses and
plushy padded strollers. I never had a stroller
for Grace, and she slept in a big dresser
drawer until Mama left, and then she moved
into my bed. She's still there, snoring and
grinding her teeth and sometimes having
nightmares and wetting the bed.

Grace and I had a Mamaw and Papaw
Wish Book, too. We never had any grandparents because Mama's family died in a car
crash before we were born and Pa's parents
lived down south. So Grace and I cut old
people from the Sears catalog, all with shining silver hair and rosy cheeks.

Out of all the Wish Books, my favorite
was my Horse Wish Book. It was all mine
because Grace had no interest in horses, only
doll babies. I didn't need doll babies. I had
Grace.

I've loved horses ever since I was knee-
high to a Shetland pony, Pa says. Only trouble was, we could never afford a horse. Pa's
paycheck covered the trailer and lot rent,
groceries, telephone, and sometimes the elec-

tric bill. Anything that was left over went
into Pa's old pickup truck.

The Horse Wish Book was pink because
there was nothing in the world I wanted
more than a strawberry roan pony. I'd cut a
picture of one from a magazine in Doc Jeffries' office and glued it to the cover of the
pink notebook. The rest of the horses in my
Horse Wish Book were pencil sketches,
which I'd been working on for years. They
were pretty good, I must admit, but that
strawberry roan on the cover took the cake.
The pony was running against the wind, its
sleek brown coat streaked with pink and glistening in the sunlight. It was the most magnificent creature I'd ever seen in my life.

"If wishes were dollars, we'd be rich," I
said to Grace. She just nodded and squirted
a big glob of paste on the back of a lady
swirling in green satin and a circle of pearls.
The lady looked as if she didn't have a care
in the world.

I wondered if I'd look like that, if all my
wishes came true.

CHAPTER 2

Luther's Story

The electric bill hadn't been paid again, so Pa was heating bath water on the gas stove. He was grumbling and cursing up a storm, which in my opinion was quite uncalled for on a Sunday morning.

"Don't know why Flynn went and put that new water heater in," Pa growled. "All it does is eat up electric."

"He was just trying to be nice, Pa," I said. I liked Mr. Flynn, our landlord.

"If he wanted to be nice, he could have lowered the rent," Pa said. "Now *that* would be *nice*."

8

"Hurry up, Pa," Grace said, hopping up and down and wringing her hands.

I swear that child couldn't sit still or hold her tongue to save her life. "Be patient, Grace," I said. "Patience is a virtue." I felt very virtuous, dressed in white. White was my favorite color. It was pure and clean and didn't clash with my hair.

"Why is patience a Gertrude?" Grace asked, jiggling her bare foot against the kitchen cupboard.

"I said patience is a *virtue*, not a *Gertrude*." I grabbed Grace's foot and held it still. Her wiggling and jiggling drove me up a wall.

"Do you like Gertrude, Maizie?"

"She's okay. If not for Gertrude, we wouldn't have Luther." Luther was our droopy old beagle dog, and Gertrude was our snoopy old neighbor.

"Well, I don't like her. Her house smells like cabbage." Grace crinkled her nose, and I suddenly remembered Mama making the exact same expression, with her nose and forehead all scrunched up and her eyes narrow like a snake's. Grace is a heartbreaker, all right. She has this delicate little nose and big blue eyes that make you want to take a dive into them.

"Love thy neighbor," I said. I was brushing up on Scripture because I was in love with Jonathan Shepherd, the preacher's boy. Ministers' sons fancy girls who are well versed in biblical matters, so Becky Gardner says. Becky's been my best friend forever. Her father is a truck driver for Weaver's Chicken, and their house always smells like batter-dipped drumsticks and diesel fuel.

"It doesn't matter if Gertrude's house smells like cabbage or rosewater or skunkweed," I said sternly. "What matters is the person within."

My little sermon was lost on Grace, who blinked and said, "Tell me Luther's Story." Grace loved my stories, which included Luther's Story, A Tale of Two Sisters, and Rainbow Fables or Stories of Mama and the Man. My repertoire also had some fairy tales, like Sleeping Beauty and Rapunzel.

"That's for bedtime," I said, but Grace

jumped up and grabbed me around the waist.

"Okay, okay," I said, and dragged Grace's skinny little body into the living room, where we plopped down on the saggy green sofa. Pa was still waiting for the water to heat up.

"It was the coldest night of the winter," I began, and Grace shivered in her thin nightgown. I looked at her and vowed to sew that hole in the sleeve someday.

"The moon was full and the kerosene lantern was empty, so I was slopping Mrs. Porkenbean by moonlight. She was all fat and snuggled up in the straw, waiting to have her babies." I paused for dramatic effect and noticed that Pa was listening from the kitchen. He was staring at the orange and blue flame on the stove, but I could tell that he was listening. Pa reveals a lot about himself just by the way he stands and moves.

"All of a sudden, I heard a soft little whine. I knew that no pig could make a sound like that, so I poked around in the straw until I felt something soft and warm and furry all cozied up to Mrs. Porkenbean."

"And it was a puppy," Grace said, fidgeting.

"A runt of a puppy," I said. "I ran inside and grabbed Pa's flashlight and saw that it was a beagle, just like Gertrude's dog."

"If Pa had a flashlight, why didn't you use that to slop Mrs. Porkenbean?" Grace asked. That child never missed a trick. She asked the same question every time. "Why did you use the light of the moon?"

"The moon was free," I replied. "I didn't want to waste Pa's batteries."

Grace nodded. "Oh," she said, like always.

"Anyway," I continued, "the dog looked exactly like Gertrude's dog, only littler and cuter."

"It was black and brown and white, with floppy ears and a white spot on its belly that was shaped like a heart," Grace said. She picked a piece of lint off the sofa and dropped it on the floor.

"Who do you think cleans this trailer, Missy?" I asked Grace. "The maid?" I picked up the lint and put it in Pa's ashtray.

"Go on with the story," Grace said, leaning forward and twirling the ashtray in circles on the coffee table.

"Well, when I told Pa about the pup, he insisted that I run right down to Gertrude's to see if she'd claim it. So I bundled that little critter up inside my coat, and down the road we went. By the time we got to Gertrude's house, I was pretty darned attached to that whiny little runt."

Pa rubbed his eyes, and I knew he was thinking of how Grace had colic and was such a sickly little thing when she was born.

Grace frowned. "You didn't want to give the puppy back to that smelly old woman."

I ignored Grace and continued the story. "When I knocked on the door and asked Miss Gertrude if the pup belonged to her, she said it most certainly did not. She said it belonged to lazy old Lucy Fay, but that old dog was too doggone lazy to take care of her own flesh and blood and fur. So from that day on, Luther was ours."

"And Mrs. Porkenbean's," Grace said quickly. She knew all my stories by heart.

"And Mrs. Porkenbean's," I agreed. "Mrs. Porkenbean gave birth to some mighty fine swine that night, but out of all her babies, Luther was her favorite. She cared for him as if he were a squirmy little pink piglet . . . as if he were her very own."

Grace took a deep breath. "And the moral of the story is . . ."

"That anyone can take a baby and love it like a mama does and make it their own," I said. Grace usually didn't want to hear about morals.

"Just like you took care of me when I was a baby," Grace said, looking up at me with her cornflower-blue eyes.

I looked at Pa and he looked at me, then we both looked at Grace. "Just like that," I said, hoping Grace and I wouldn't be late for church.

CHAPTER 3

Brother Roe's Announcement

I was sitting in the third pew, staring at the back of Jonathan Shepherd's head. He had the shiniest black hair I'd ever seen. It reminded me of Becky's black onyx ring when it shimmered in the sunlight. Pa had black hair, too, but his was more like a chunk of heated coal. I wondered if Pa's hair would shine if he would attend church.

I used to wonder if Pa ever prayed. I figured he didn't, because the Bible says that if you ask for something you'll receive it. I'd been waiting for four years and still hadn't received a new mama or even had my old one returned to me. I reckoned that Pa had never put in his request, because the Lord surely has a lot of mamas to spare. I prayed for one every night, but maybe God couldn't hear me over Grace's snoring.

Pa only talked about The Leaving one time, when he'd been drinking. "I didn't want her to go, Maizie," he said. "I told her that if she'd stay, I'd give her my heart on a silver platter." He'd swallowed hard and continued. "She just said, 'You can't give away what you don't have, Jake.' And then she walked out the door."

For some reason, the thought of Pa cutting out his heart and presenting it to Mama on a silver platter tickled my funny bone that Sunday morning. I started to shake all over like Pa's old pickup truck when he's trying to start it. I coughed and sputtered and hoped that Jonathan Shepherd wouldn't hear me. He didn't, but his mother did.

Mrs. Shepherd turned around and looked at me. She was wearing pink lipstick and cinnamon-colored eye shadow and a flowered dress. She smiled at me, and she was the most beautiful lady I ever saw. I decided that when I was a mother, I'd get me some shiny lipstick and spicy eye shadow and a billowy white dress with gardenias on it. And that I'd never run off and leave my babies behind. I also decided that if anything should ever happen to Pastor John, I wouldn't mind having Mrs. Shepherd for a mama.

Pastor John was preaching about salvation, and Jonathan was staring straight ahead, obviously listening to his daddy's sermon in deep concentration. That was one of the things I liked about Jonathan Shepherd, the way he respected his father. I loved my Pa dearly, but I could never quite bring myself to wholeheartedly respect him, with all the drinking and smoking and cussing he did. He said that he drank on Saturday nights to scare the coming week away, he smoked because of his bad nerves, and it was none of my business how he talked.

Pa and I had a nasty squabble before church about my Strawberry Roan Donation Can, which I put on the kitchen table for Aunt Virginia's Sunday visit. Aunt Virginia was rolling in money, and I knew she wouldn't mind donating to my horse fund, so I decorated an empty coffee can with the Sunday funnies and wrote in black marker: PLEASE DONATE TO MAIZIE MUS-SER'S STRAWBERRY ROAN PONY FUND. YOUR KIND CONTRIBU-TIONS ARE GREATLY APPRECI-ATED. THANK YOU VERY MUCH.

I thought I did a good job with tasteful decorating and polite wording, but Pa dis-agreed. He said that it made us look like spongers to his only sister, the great Virginia from West Virginia. She moved to Pennsyl-vania after her divorce, with a lot of gold jewelry, a little red car, and a voice like soft taffy.

Pa said that Virginia faked her southern drawl, but I was sure it was real. She always referred to Luther as a "bagel" instead of a beagle. It made me laugh to think of Luther being one of those hard doughnut-shaped things I hear they eat in New York City with cream cheese.

Aunt Virginia called everybody "sugar"

and said "I do declare" a lot. Pa said it was because Virginia wanted us hardened mountain people to think of her as a soft southern belle. He called her The Milk Toast Lady and she called him The Man of Steel.

Pa and Virginia were a typical brother and sister, always ribbing one another. They put me in mind of Grace and myself, the way they picked at each other. Grace was a pain in my neck, but when it came right down to it, I knew that I'd walk through fire for her. I guess that's how a mama is supposed to feel. I was the closest thing to a mama Grace ever had, except the first ten months of her life, and Grace doesn't remember anything about that time. Shoot, Grace doesn't even remember yesterday.

I was glad when Grace went downstairs to children's church instead of staying in the sanctuary with the adults. Once, when she stayed and took communion, she was a holy terror. She begged for another piece of bread, then asked Pastor John if the grape juice was really beer. I was never so embarrassed in my life.

Even though she drove me crazy, I had the patience of Job with Grace. I didn't snap out at her or ignore her the way Pa did at times. I think that, deep down inside, Pa blamed Grace for The Leaving. Maybe he thought that Mama wouldn't have left if Grace hadn't been such a crybaby.

Pastor John was asking for prayer requests. Dory Fisher, who was almost as wide as she was tall, stood up and asked for strength and willpower. Wilbur Jones asked for prayer for his son in jail, and Clyde Bolens asked for guidance in his farm equipment business. I had some prayer requests, but I wasn't about to stand up in view of the entire congregation, so I made my requests inside myself.

"Lord," I said, "I have three main requests, if that's not being too greedy. Number one, I'd like to ask for a mama. Preferably, my old one will come home, but if that's not possible, please send a new one. Any color hair will be fine, but she should like kids and animals. My second request is for a strawberry roan pony, as you already know. I'm sure you heard Pa say that Mussers are not moochers and that I wasn't allowed to display my donation can on the table. Well, I don't expect you to just send a pony flying through the skies to me, but I do need a way to buy one. Please supply the funds. And last, I wouldn't mind having a set of grandparents. I need somebody to help out with Grace every now and then. Thank you very much, Lord." I didn't ask for the baby brother because I was afraid that the Lord would wonder why on earth I wanted another baby when I needed help with Grace. And that was a question I couldn't really answer.

When I opened my eyes, I noticed that Brother Roe was standing. "I'd like to make an announcement," he bellowed. Brother Roe always liked to make announcements. He had a red face and a permanent case of static cling and ring around the collar. Brother Roe was a living laundry-soap commercial.

"The Blue Moon Nursing Home, over on Spooky Nook Road, is looking for students between the ages of twelve and sixteen to assist with the care of the elderly. It's a summer job and pays minimum wage. Those interested may see me after the service. As most of you know, my mother is a Blue Moon resident." Brother Roe cleared his throat and sat down.

After the service, I moseyed up to Brother Roe. "I have two questions," I said to him. "When can I start, and what does 'minimum wage' mean?"

CHAPTER 4

The Milk Toast Lady and The Man of Steel

Pa and I were making chicken corn soup for Sunday supper, and I was trying not to think about how the chicken in the pot used to peck around in our backyard and answer to the name of Irma.

"So tell me, what in tarnation is a moon-striper?" Pa asked, opening a can of corn with his pocketknife.

"It's the name that Blue Moon Nursing Home gives to the employees who help out with the old folks," I explained. "Back when you were a kid, Pa, they were called candy stripers. I guess that Blue Moon thought they'd be cute and change the name. You have to admit, moonstriper does sound kind of exciting." I dumped the corn in the pot.

Pa shook his head. "Sounds like somebody who paints lines around the moon."

"If I can manage to paint the moon, I can do anything on this earth," I said.

Pa didn't say anything. He stirred the soup with one hand and lit a cigarette from the gas flame with the other.

"I hate when you do that, Pa."

He still didn't answer, just puffed away and stirred the soup.

"If I worked as a moonstriper, I could save my money for a strawberry roan," I said. "You know that's my heart's desire," I added, trying to sound like daddy's little girl. Becky says that whenever she wants something, all she has to do is pout and talk in a syrupy voice as she bats her eyelids and she gets anything she wants. She calls it being daddy's little girl. That was how she got her black onyx ring and pierced ears. When I asked Pa for pierced ears, he said that I already had a hole in the head and what did I want two in my ears for.

"Please, Pa. Pretty please with a cherry and chocolate syrup and sprinkles on top," I said, but sweet-talking Pa is like sweet-talking a brick wall. It gets you nowhere.

"Where would you keep a horse?" he asked.

"In the barn with Mrs. Porkenbean."

"And Luther and the chickens and Wooly Girl," Pa said, and looked out the kitchen window at the little barn on the back of our lot. "Anyway, that barn needs painting." It was the color of a faded old rubber eraser.

"I'll do it," I said.

"And how would a horse manage among all those other animals?"

"It would get to be a very smart horse," I said. "It would learn how to bark and lay eggs and mow the yard." Wooly Girl was a sheep who thought she was a lawn mower.

"Luther and the chickens and Mrs. Porkenbean and Wooly Girl all serve practical purposes," Pa said. "What practical purpose would a horse serve?"

"Transportation," I said. "And it would make me happy."

The Man of Steel didn't even crack a smile. "Speaking of transportation, how would you get to Blue Moon?"

"I'd walk. It's not far, only a stone's throw across the mountain to Spooky Nook Road."

"I thought you were scared of Spooky Nook Road," Pa said.

I sighed. "That was when I was a kid, Pa."

"And what about your schoolwork?"

"It's a summer job," I said. "And it would be educational, working with the old folks." I knew that would get him. Pa placed great importance on education. He wanted better for me and Grace than he had for himself. He was always saying that education was the ticket to a better place.

Pa nodded and stubbed out his cigarette. "Reckon it would be an education, dumping bedpans and wiping bottoms and spooning pablum," he said. "How would you like helping people who can't help themselves?"

"I've done it with Grace for four years," I said.

Pa sighed. "Can't argue with that," he said. "Speaking of Grace, who'd watch her while you were at work?"

"Kelly and Dory Fisher," I said, shrugging my shoulders. "Grace is with them all the time, anyway, when I'm in school." Dory Fisher didn't work because of her health problems, and Kelly was trying to save money for college.

"I didn't plan on paying a baby-sitter for the summer," Pa complained.

"But think of all the money you'll save next year, Pa, when Grace starts school," I said.

Pa took a deep breath, then sighed. "I guess it would suit you just fine, taking care of old folks. You have a lot of patience."

"That I do, Pa, or I couldn't put up with you." I grinned and added, "Some of the money from my job could help pay the electric bill."

Pa's eyes softened like butter in the oven, and he shifted his weight. That always meant yes. "Okay, Miss Maizie Moonstriper," he grumbled. "But you'd best get

rid of that confounded coffee can. Mussers
are not moochers."

The Man of Steel had melted.

Aunt Virginia breezed through the door
just as we were sitting down to supper.
"Hello, hello," she drawled, and planted a
kiss on my cheek.

"How's life treating you, baby brother?"
she asked, grabbing Pa in a bear hug. It was
hard to imagine Pa being anybody's baby
brother, least of all Virginia's.

"No use complaining," Pa said. "Nobody
listens anyway."

"I do," Grace said.

"Gracie-poo!" Aunt Virginia squealed like
a stuck pig. "Give me some sugar." When
she bent down to give Grace a miniature bear
hug, I saw that she'd dyed her hair a new
shade of blonde. Aunt Virginia said that
blondes have more fun, and judging from
her, I'd have to agree.

"Take a load off your feet and have some
Irma stew with us," Pa said.

I put down my spoon. "Pa!" I complained.

"Watch your mouth." Grace wouldn't eat anything that used to have eyes.

Grace tugged on Aunt Virginia's bracelet-bedecked arm. "Eat with us," she said.

"No, thank you, sugar," Aunt Virginia said, patting her stomach. "Must watch my figure if I expect anyone else to."

"Say grace, Grace," I said.

Grace bowed her head, and with half-closed eyes she said, "Good soup, good meat, good God, let's eat."

"Grace!" I said. "I taught you better than that."

Pa snickered and I turned on him. "And you, Pa! Where's your head, teaching an innocent child to sass the Lord."

"Oh, Maizie, Grace, how sweet the sound," Aunt Virginia sang in a screechy soprano. She was crazy as a coot, that aunt of mine. Her and Pa are as different as molasses and cauliflower. You'd never catch Pa monkeyshining around like Virginia does. Aunt Virginia is footloose and fancy-free. Pa is down-in-the-mouth, downhearted, and downright depressing most of the time. The only song Pa ever sings is the blues.

"You'd never make a church choir girl, Virginia," Pa said. "You can't even carry a tune into the backyard."

Later, after the dishes were done and I'd finally gotten Grace to sleep, Aunt Virginia and I were alone in the kitchen. I didn't know where Pa had run off to, but I was glad he was gone, because I'd been wanting to ask Aunt Virginia some questions. The kind of questions I'd never ask Pa. The kind I always asked Aunt Virginia.

"Why do you think Mama left?" I asked for the hundredth time as I poured Aunt Virginia a cup of black coffee. She runs on coffee the way her little red car runs on gasoline.

"I don't really know, Maizie. I don't think your mother even knew." It wasn't like Virginia not to know the answer to a question, but that was the reply I got every time I asked.

"Well, just guess, Aunt Virginia. Why do you guess she left?"

Aunt Virginia ran her fingers through her

hair and smiled. "I reckon that maybe she wanted a little more color in her life and that's why she chose the Rainbow man over The Man of Steel," she said.

"You don't think she left because of me and Grace?"

"I think she left in spite of you and Grace," said Aunt Virginia, and we both were quiet for a minute.

"Sugar, she loved you girls. You should have seen her face the night you were born. I never saw a face with so much love in it." Aunt Virginia sipped her coffee. "They say that giving birth is the sweetest experience of womanhood. I wouldn't know."

There was something I'd been wondering about lately, and I decided it was now or never. If Aunt Virginia didn't know the answer, nobody did. "How do you know when you're a woman?" I asked.

Aunt Virginia choked on her coffee and reached over to hold my hand. Her fingernails glistened pearly pink in the glow of the kerosene lantern. "You been feeling kind of funny inside lately, darlin'?"

I nodded. "Inside and outside. I feel like a kid who's near being an adult . . . or an adult who's not over being a kid. Sort of caught in the middle. Do you know what I mean?"

Aunt Virginia smiled. "Are you moody sometimes?"

"I bet I change my moods as often as you change your earrings," I said.

Aunt Virginia laughed, twisting one of her silvery star earrings. She had two holes in the left ear and four in the right. "Do you ever have trouble making up your mind?" she asked.

"Aunt Virginia, I'm so full of wants and don't wants that I don't know what I do want," I said.

"Welcome to womanhood," she said. "And Maizie . . ." She stopped to trace the rim of her coffee cup. "You don't have to grow up all alone. You do have me."

Before she left, Aunt Virginia slipped something into my donation can, which Pa had hidden on top of the refrigerator. "A little something for the strawberry roan fund," she whispered. "Just don't tell The Man of Steel."

"Don't worry," I said as I watched her little red car disappear into the night. "I won't."

CHAPTER 5

Upside-down Hearts

I was at Becky's house, playing Hoss with Becky and her parents. Hoss is a card game Becky learned from her mother, who learned it from *her* mother. Mrs. Gardner said that it used to be called Hossipepper, back in the days before everybody was in such a hurry.

We were sipping iced tea with slices of real lemon and snacking on seedless grapes, banana coins, and chunks of apple. Mrs. Gardner had arranged all the fruit on a thing called a lazy Susan. You spin it and it goes around like a roulette wheel, with four half-moon shaped bowls surrounding one big round one. In the middle bowl, there were hunks of cheese with yellow fish crackers swimming between them. When Becky comes to my house, I just drag a bag of potato chips and a couple of cans of cola into the bedroom, and we have to share with Grace. At the Gardners', you don't have to share with anybody but yourself.

"Anybody for some cashews?" Mrs. Gardner asked, pouring a pile of nuts into a bowl.

"What?" asked Mr. Gardner.

"Cashews," said Mrs. Gardner.

"Bless you," Mr. Gardner said.

"Oh, you," said Mrs. Gardner, digging him in the ribs. "I didn't sneeze."

They're always like that, clowning around and cracking jokes as if life is just one big circus.

"Hearts are trump," said Mrs. Gardner, scooping a handful of cashews from the bowl. Mrs. Gardner is plump and wears a lot of polyester, but something about her makes her prettier than most mothers. She has a kind of glow about her.

"Our trick," Becky said, taking all the cards from the middle of the yellow and white cotton tablecloth. At home, we used an oilcloth because it was easier to wipe clean. Also, we used paper towels rather than monogrammed cloth napkins like the Gardners had. We were just a different kind of family from the Gardners, I guess.

Becky was the only friend I had who'd known me before and after The Leaving. She knew that I'd never heard from Mama since she moved to Pittsburgh and that I'd never seen the Rainbow man, only the back of his bald head as he drove away in his big black car with my mama. Becky knew that Pa drank and that Grace wet the bed and that I had a stack of Wish Books stashed in the back of the closet. She knew that I was in love with Jonathan Shepherd and that I couldn't stand Brother Roe. She knew that I couldn't remember very much about the woman who'd been my mama for eight years: Ruby Lou Musser. For all I knew, her name was now Ruby Lou Rainbow.

"Stop daydreaming, Maizie," Becky

scolded. Becky always took games too seriously.

"I wasn't daydreaming," I said. "I was considering which card to use."

"Diamonds are trump now," Becky said. I couldn't see her eyes behind her glasses, but Becky likes it that way when she's playing Hoss. She's always afraid that somebody is going to cheat. So is Grace, but that's probably a childhood scar from our mama's adultery.

"Diamonds are a girl's best friend," sang Mr. Gardner. He's big and jolly and reminds me of the Kmart Santa Claus.

"Daddy, could I get diamond earrings someday?" Becky asked, her voice sticky with sweetness. She pouted and batted her eyes.

"Someday, sweetheart," Mr. Gardner said. Maybe he really was Santa, the way he always got Becky just what she wanted. Becky said it was because he made big bucks hauling chicken, but I'd never heard of anybody making that much money. After all, black onyx rings, diamond earrings, and slick satin bedspreads like Becky had on her canopy bed couldn't be bought at Charlie's Cut Rate.

"And how about a matching necklace?" Becky had taken off her glasses, and her eyes were batting a thousand. Daddy's little girl strikes again.

"Maybe, sweetheart." Mr. Gardner shuffled the cards.

"I'd be happy just to have matching socks," I said, and they all laughed. But I wasn't joking. "Our old wringer washing machine eats socks and underwear, and sometimes arms."

"Did you like the chicken, Maizie?" asked Mrs. Gardner. For supper, she'd served up a new Weaver's product called Zesty Wings.

"Yes, ma'am," I said. "Thank you."

Mr. and Mrs. Gardner traded a look, and I knew that they were both thinking the same thing—what a polite, mature, grown-up young lady I was. If only they knew that I'd swiped one of their family photographs and cut out Mrs. Gardner for my Mama Wish Book.

"Your bid, Maizie," Becky said. "By the way, Mother, the mashed potatoes were awfully lumpy tonight." Becky didn't appreciate her mama at all, which exasperated me.

"I bid five," I said, spinning the lazy Susan and helping myself to a grape. Mrs. Gardner had all the grape stems turned the same direction. Too bad that life wasn't as neat and orderly and seedless as those perfectly arranged grapes, I thought, as I snatched a fistful of fish crackers.

"Upside-down hearts are trump," said Mrs. Gardner.

"What on earth are upside-down hearts, Mother?" asked Becky, sucking on the lemon from her iced tea.

"Spades," Mrs. Gardner said. "Didn't you ever notice that they're black, upside-down hearts?"

Mr. Gardner laughed. "Those upside-down hearts are worth just as much as any other card in the deck," he said.

Later that night, when I was snuggled up in bed trying not to listen to Grace's snoring, I thought of how those upside-down hearts were like my family. Pa, Grace, and I were all topsy-turvy, bumbling around in a world of other people's diamonds and perfect hearts.

I contemplated how growing up means feeling funny inside, as if your heart has turned upside-down and your emotions inside-out.

And then I heard Mr. Gardner's deep voice again, saying that upside-down hearts are worth as much as any other card in the deck.

I hugged Sed, the dirt-brown teddy bear I'd had since I was two. Sed was missing one leg, two eyes, and an ear. "You're lucky you don't have a heart to worry about, Seddy," I whispered in his only ear. Then I nudged Grace and rolled her over so that she'd stop snoring.

"Anyway," I said, partly to myself and partly to Sed, "anything that's upside-down can right itself, you know. All it takes is time, and patience. And patience is the one thing I have a lot of. Good things are worth waiting for."

"What did you say, Maizie?" Grace mumbled.

"I said patience is a virtue, Grace."

"I don't like Gertrude. Good night, Maizie." Grace reached over and snitched my pillow.

"Good night, Grace," I said.

Sed, Grace, and I drifted off to sleep, but not before I heard the screen door bang shut with a sound like a harmonica chord.

CHAPTER 6

Endings and Beginnings

"Where'd you go last night, Pa?" I asked.

Pa ran his hand through his hair, which was all sweaty and rumpled from his welding helmet. "When?" he asked, not looking at me.

"When Grace and I were in bed," I replied. "I heard the screen door."

"What are you doing, Maizie, writing a book?" Pa always said that when he didn't want to answer a question.

"Someday," I said.

"Someday is a long way away," Pa grumbled, putting his lunchpail in the sink. When

Pa came home from work, everything was covered with a fine black dust.

"Really, Pa, where'd you go?" I washed off his lunchpail.

Pa still wouldn't look at me. "Down to Doc Jeffries," he mumbled. "What's for supper?"

"Are you sick, Pa?" I imagined Pa's lungs coated with a fine black dust, just like his lunchpail.

"I'm healthy as a horse, Maizie. What's for supper?"

I lifted my hair off my neck. "Too hot to cook, Pa. You know how the trailer heats up like an oven in the summertime." Actually, I was too excited to cook. Pa was getting a promotion and a raise, it was my last day of school, and Jonathan Shepherd's mama was going to be baby-sitting Grace for the summer, rather than the Fishers. Mrs. Shepherd was opening a kind of Christian day-care center in her home.

"Let's go down to Nino's and get a pizza, Pa. In celebration of beginnings and endings."

"Beginnings and endings?" Pa repeated.

"We're all beginning something tomorrow," I explained. "I'm beginning my new job at Blue Moon, Grace is beginning to have Mrs. Shepherd as her baby-sitter, and you're beginning your new career, welding crushers instead of conveyor belts." Pa worked underground, in the iron ore mine.

"Career, huh?" Pa said. "And what about the endings?"

"I'm ending another year of school, you're ending fifteen years on your old job, and Grace is ending the Fishers as her baby-sitters."

Grace clung to Pa's dirty pantlegs. "I'm glad that Kelly and Dory aren't baby-sitting me anymore. All Kelly cares about is boys, and all Dory cares about is diets."

"You'll like staying with Mrs. Shepherd," I said. "They have a big house with a playroom, a color television set, and a microwave oven that'll bake you a potato quicker than you can say, 'Sour cream and chives.' "

Grace looked at me sideways. "And

Jonathan Shepherd," she said. "All you care about is boys."

"All I care about is you," I said. "And Pa."

"All you care about is Jonathan Shepherd and getting a mama and baby brother and a mamaw and papaw and a raspberry roan pony," Grace said in one breath.

"A strawberry roan pony," I corrected her.

"Strawberry, raspberry, all the same," Pa said. "I think you're both fruity."

Grace and I looked at each other. "Pa made a joke," Grace said, her eyes wide.

"I'm in a good mood tonight," Pa said. "Let's go fetch that pizza."

Pa went to change his clothes (his work clothes are all dotted with little holes from welding sparks), and I dipped his thermos in the dishwater. "Grace, get me the denture cleaner, would you, please?" I scratched my nose with a soapy finger.

"What's denture cleaner, Maizie?"

"It's in the bottom cupboard," I said. "A

blue and white box with a picture of false teeth soaking in a cup."

"Do you have fake teeth like Mr. Gardner, Maizie?" Grace asked. Becky's father had chased Grace with his choppers once, pretending they were going to bite her. She'd had nightmares about walking teeth for weeks after.

"No, Grace. My teeth are as real as the hair on your head." I tugged on one of her black pigtails. Grace has Pa's looks and Mama's personality. I have Mama's looks and my own personality.

"What are you doing with this stuff, then?" She handed me the box.

"Cleaning Pa's coffee thermos." I dropped a white cleaning tablet into Pa's tall metal thermos, filled it with water, and watched it fizz for a while.

"How do you figure everything out, Maizie?"

"Like what?" I shook the thermos and poured the blue liquid down the drain. Chunks of hardened black coffee chugged out along with the denture cleaner. I discovered when I was ten that denture cleaner will also clean a coffee thermos. After all, the directions on the box read, "Strong against stubborn stains." And there's nothing more stubborn than Pa's coffee thermos, except maybe Pa.

"How do you figure out things like cooking and cleaning and washing clothes and fixing a fence?" I'd repaired the barbed-wire fence that kept Wooly Girl and the chickens in our yard.

"The same way a blind person figures out which way to go," I told Grace. "By feeling my way through the dark."

Pa, Grace, and I crowded into the pickup, and Grace leaned over and honked the horn. That was Luther's signal that he was allowed to go along. Grace hung across me and yelled out the window, "Come on, Luther! Go bye-byes." Luther waddled across the yard, his ears flopping. That dog was so fat from table scraps.

Luther stood in back of the truck and whined until Pa got out and heaved him into the bed.

"You're getting as lazy as your mother, old Lucy Fay," Pa said.

Luther scampered to the end of the truck bed and, panting, looked in the back window at us.

"At least Wooly Girl doesn't think she can go along," Grace said. Not only did Wooly Girl think she was a lawn mower—she also thought she was a dog. She'd spent so much time with Luther that she'd taken to jumping up on the back door of the trailer, like Luther did when he wanted to come inside. The door had dents all over it from Wooly Girl's hooves.

"It's bad enough that the dumb dog thinks he can go," Pa said. "Stupid mutt." That was Pa's way of saying that he loved Luther. Pa never could come right out and say, "I love you." It probably would have stuck in his throat like a chicken bone.

Pa pumped the gas pedal, and the engine growled and groaned, but the truck finally started. It coughed and sputtered as we rattled up the stone driveway and turned onto Mountain Road.

"This truck reminds me of Gertrude," Grace said. "The way it's always coughing and spitting."

Pa snorted through his nose. That was how Pa laughed.

"Now that you got a raise, are you going to fix the door?" Grace asked. The door on the passenger side never shut all the way, so Grace always had to sit in the middle, which she hated because of the gearshift.

Pa just shrugged.

I thought of how Pa would be mad as a wet hen if he knew that Aunt Virginia had taken me out on Mountain Road in his truck and taught me to shift gears. Pa was passed out on the sofa when Aunt Virginia sneaked the keys from his pocket. "You need to learn to drive, Maizie," she said. "You never know when you might have a need to get from here to there."

Aunt Virginia said that I did real good because not a lot of girls knew how to drive with a stick shift. The only trouble I had was getting that old truck from first into reverse.

"I lost a tooth today, Pa," Grace said.

Pa nodded and stared straight ahead at the winding road. He never cared much about teeth. When Mama first left, I lost a tooth and put it under my pillow like I always did before The Leaving. The next morning, the tooth was still there, coated with dried blood. When I asked Pa why I didn't get a dime, he said that the Tooth Fairy had flown away and been hit by an airplane. He also said that the Easter Bunny had been bagged by a hunter and that Santa Claus was in prison. I didn't believe him at the time, but since then I think he might be right.

"I have the tooth in my pocket, Pa," Grace said.

Pa nodded again. A thunderstorm was brewing down in the valley. Smoky black clouds rolled in and lightning rippled the sky.

"That's God moving his furniture," Grace said as thunder rumbled and rain pelted down on the truck. "Now He's draining His bathtub," she added.

The road was slick as a greased pig and Pa hadn't slowed the truck. As we careened down the mountain and whipped around a sharp turn, I glanced in the side mirror and saw Luther land on the road like a lost sack of potatoes.

"Stop, Pa!" I hollered. "Luther."

Pa slammed on the brakes and we skidded to the side of the road.

Pa, Grace, and I tumbled from the truck and ran to where Luther lay limply in the middle of the road.

"Luther's dead," Grace sobbed.

"No, he's not," Pa snapped, bending down and lifting Luther like a baby. Lightning brightened the sky and Pa's eyes were wet. It could have been from the rain, but it sure did look like Pa was crying. "Get in the truck," he said to me and Grace.

Grace and I climbed in, and Pa slumped behind the wheel. He handed Luther to me. "We best forget about the pizza," Pa said. "Stupid mutt looks like a drowned rat," he added, but nobody laughed.

When we got home, Pa looked Luther over and said that he had a broken leg. He fixed a splint from some plywood and rags.

"You should have been a veterinarian, Pa, not a welder," I said.

"Should-have-beens don't count," Pa said, and rubbed his eyes. He bundled Luther in an old blanket that Grace used to carry around. "He'll sleep inside tonight," Pa said.

When Grace and I went to bed, Pa stopped by the doorway. "You forgot to turn off the bathroom light, Maizie," he grumbled. "You have stock in the electric company?" Whenever the electricity was turned back on, Pa watched that meter like a hawk. Grace and I had to take a bath together, and we were allowed to run hot water only for five minutes. Also, I had to use a wire whisk instead of the electric mixer, and no hair dryers or curling irons were allowed in our house. I blamed the unruliness of my hair and the lumpiness of my chocolate pudding on these facts. "Sorry, Pa. I'll try to do better," I said.

"Now that you're going to be helping with the electric bill, you will do better," Pa muttered, stroking the black stubble on his chin. "Oh, and Grace," he said as he walked away.

"Tuck that tooth under your pillow. I heard a rumor that the Tooth Fairy is starting back to work tonight."

Grace and I looked at each other. "How much money do you think I'll get, Maizie?" Grace asked.

"Money is the root of all evil," I said.

Grace wrinkled her brow. "Then why are you getting a job?" she asked.

I just shrugged, but I knew the reason. It was that magnificent brown and pink pony galloping across the cover of my Wish Book.

Pa reappeared in the doorway. "I'm frying up some eggs and scrapple, if anybody's interested," he said. "We were all so worked up about the dumb dog that we forgot supper."

Grace and I sat up. "It surely was a day full of endings and beginnings," I said as we headed for the kitchen.

None of us knew that the next day, too, would be one for beginnings . . . and endings.

CHAPTER 7

Stupid Mutt

The next morning, Luther was dead. I found him still as night, wrapped in that old baby quilt. "Pa!" I called. "Pa, come quick!" My voice was too loud in the trailer.

Pa stumbled from his room, his eyes heavy with sleep. "What are you trying to do, Maizie, wake the dead?"

My look must have told him everything, because he stopped cold in the hallway. "No," he said. "No."

"He's gone, Pa. Luther is gone."

"Maybe not," he snapped. "Get a cold cloth."

"That's not going to help, Pa," I began, but the look on Pa's face hushed me. He looked tired and old and white, like stale bread that might crumble if you touch it. "Be right back," I said, and ran to the bathroom for a washcloth.

"What are you doing, Maizie?" Grace was standing in the hall, her hair tousled and her cheeks sheet-creased. "I got a dollar from the Tooth Fairy." She clutched a crumpled dollar bill in her hand.

I ignored her and dashed out to the living room, the cloth dripping. "Where are you going, Maizie?" Grace whined.

"It's too late, Maizie," Pa said quietly. "Stupid mutt's gone." He had completely covered Luther with the pink and white quilt.

"Gone like Mama?" Grace asked. "To Pittsburgh?"

I looked at Pa, who was slouched on the sofa with his hands over his face.

"He died, Grace," I said. "Luther died in his sleep last night." I bit the inside of my cheek to keep from crying.

Grace fixed those blue eyes on me. "Why?" she asked.

I took a deep breath and glanced at Pa, who didn't look as if he was going to be any help. "Guess it was just his time," I said.

"But Luther couldn't tell time," Grace said.

I put my arm around her. "The Lord knew it was Luther's time. He just loaned Luther to us for a little while, and then it was time for us to give Luther back."

Understanding flooded Grace's face, and she nodded. "Just like when I borrowed a book from the library?" she asked.

I smiled. "Just like that," I said.

Grace furrowed her brow. "But I thought that Pa said Luther only had a broken leg and he'd be okay."

I looked at Pa, who hadn't budged. "Luther was hurt on the inside, where nobody can see," I said. "That's called an internal injury."

"Pa should have been going slower down the mountain," Grace said.

Help me out, Pa, I pleaded silently.

"Should-have-beens don't count, Grace," I said.

Pa looked up, and there were dark circles under his eyes. "Come on, girls," he said. "Let's give Luther a proper burial."

We went outside, Grace and I still in our nightgowns and Pa in his holey work pants and bare feet. A warm fine mist was falling.

"God is crying," Grace said. She gazed at me. "So is Maizie," she added.

"Run inside for a marker," Pa said to Grace. "And Maizie, you get Luther."

Luther felt heavy and awkward in my arms, the way Grace used to feel after Mama left. I carried him outside into the backyard.

Pa was digging a hole, his back rigid and his shoulders hunched. "Lay him down," he said.

Grace stood beside Pa, the black marker clenched in her fist. "Now I lay him down to sleep, I pray the Lord his soul to keep. If he should die before he wakes, I pray the Lord his soul to take," she said, reciting the prayer I'd taught her as soon as she could talk. "Amen," she added.

"Amen," I said, gently placing Luther in the ground. I handed the baby quilt to Grace.

"He can keep it," she said. "I don't need it anymore." She leaned over and carefully covered Luther with the worn blanket.

Without a word, Pa took the marker from Grace and wrote something on the piece of plywood Luther had worn as a splint. Then he pulled out his pocketknife and cut the piece of thin wood in half. "Get me the hammer and a nail," he said to Grace, who took off running for the barn.

Pa and I didn't look at each other as we waited in the rain for Grace's return. When she finally got back and handed Pa his hammer and a box of nails, he put the two pieces of plywood together in the shape of a cross and slowly hammered a nail into the middle. LUTHER, he had written on the horizontal piece of wood. The upright part read, REST IN PEACE.

"What are you doing, Pa?" Grace asked as he pushed the cross into the mud. "What's that for?"

"To remember Luther," Pa said.

Grace stared at him. "How could we ever forget him?" she asked.

Pa sighed. "The mind has a way of pushing sad things away, Grace," he said. "Things that hurt too much to remember."

I broke the silence. "Let's each say one good thing about Luther," I said. "You start, Grace."

She gnawed on her fingernail. "He had a white spot on his belly shaped like a heart," she finally said.

I nodded. "He was a good guard dog," I said.

Pa took a long, slow breath. "He was a fair hunting dog," he said. "Sniffed out more squirrels than any other beagle on the mountain." He rubbed his eyes. "And we all loved him," Pa said. "Stupid mutt."

As we trudged back toward the trailer, Pa's face glistened with what could have been teardrops, raindrops, or both. I watched him from behind, and from the way he moved, I could tell that Pa suffered from some sore internal injuries of his own.

"You should have been wearing shoes, Pa," I said. "You'll catch a chill in your bones."

"Should-have-beens don't count, Maizie," Pa said as he wiped the drops from his eyes and went to his bedroom to finish getting ready for work.

CHAPTER 8

Maizie Moonstriper

"You must be Maizie Musser!" The voice drifted through the blue door.

"My name is Chris Sunrise," said the voice, which sounded like a plucked banjo string. "You'll be working with me today."

The door swung open and I saw a tall woman with a long braid of pitch-black hair and a complexion the color of honey. With my red hair, I was naturally pale, and Grace didn't have any color in her cheeks because she didn't eat enough meat. Pa was white as a ghost from spending most of the daylight hours underground. So I could hardly help myself from gawking at the woman, whose name tag read, CHRIS SUNRISE, R.N.

"Is something wrong?" asked the woman.

"I'm sorry for staring," I stammered. "It's just that I don't see many people get so tanned on this mountain."

She laughed. "I'm part Navajo Indian," she said. "My father, Joe Sunrise, was a bull rider on the rodeo circuit, and Mom was a barrel racer. They were both wild and crazy."

"Are they still?" I asked. "Wild and crazy?"

"Mom retired to raising horses, rather than racing them," she said. "And Daddy died last year."

"I'm sorry," I stammered again. I always manage to stick my foot in my mouth. "My beagle dog, Luther, died this morning." Just saying his name caused something sharp to stab me inside. All morning, as I walked to Blue Moon, thoughts of Luther had churned around inside my stomach like clothes in the washing machine.

The woman's dark eyes widened. "I'm so

sorry," she said. "I know what it's like to lose a pet."

I tried to smile and struggled for something to say. I have a knack for making a fool of myself in strange situations, which I blame on Mama's not sticking around long enough to teach me all the social graces. "Thank you," I finally said. Pa had taught me that much.

Chris Sunrise smiled and handed me a name tag. It was blue, with thin white stripes and the words MAIZIE MUSSER, MOONSTRIPER.

"What size do you wear?" Chris asked, leading the way through the lobby to a closet stuffed with uniforms.

"Five," I said. "I'm skinny but strong, and I work hard."

Chris grinned and handed me a white uniform with tiny blue pinstripes marching up and down the skirt. "Put this on and you're ready to shoot for the moon," she said.

Chris showed me into the ladies' room, which was a soft powdery blue and lined with glittery mirrors. Our bathroom at home was sort of a frying-grease yellow, and the mirror was cracked. I'd never seen such a glamorous bathroom.

I squirmed into the uniform and slipped on the squishy white shoes I'd borrowed from Aunt Virginia. Luckily, she had worked as a waitress and wore the same size as me.

I stared at myself in the full-length mirror. "So that's what I look like, all in one piece," I said. If I wanted to see below my shoulders at home, I had to stand on the toilet. I'd never seen myself all in one look before.

"Maizie Musser, moonstriper," I whispered to my reflection. "It has a ring to it."

Chris Sunrise was waiting in the hall. "And now it's time for the Blue Moon Grand Tour," she said.

There was more blue than you could shake a stick at: the curtains, the shiny furniture in the lounge, the wallpaper, the door, the cafeteria trays, the toilet paper. Even the music was blue. It was the whinin' and cryin' and who's-cheatin'-on-who music that Pa listened to. He called it country music. Grace and I called it hillbilly blues.

"I feel like I'm tangled up in blue," I said as we weaved through the maze of hallways and doors.

Chris smiled and knocked on a door with a brassy blue 1 in the middle. "Time for your medication," she called, flinging open the door and striding into the room.

"This is Amelia Skiles," Chris said, and whipped open the curtains.

The lady looked up with the saddest green eyes I'd ever seen. "Please don't open the curtains," she said to Chris. "I suffer more on sunny days. The pain reflects off the air conditioner." The sun had snuck out from behind the clouds.

"Don't be silly, Amelia," Chris said.

The lady looked at me. "I've been here since my husband died two years ago," she said. "He was burying four hundred dollars the day he died. Didn't believe in banks, so he buried coffee cans filled with cash all over the yard. I liked to think of it as planting, rather than burying, in the hope that the money might grow. But still, every time I looked out the window and saw him digging a little grave, I felt like crying. To me, money is worthless until it's spent, so one time I dug up fifteen dollars and bought myself a hardcover book about President Kennedy. I never told Ben. He thought that my obsession with JFK was a waste of time. Right after he died, I dug up that four hundred dollars and bought myself a new kitchen table."

"Oh," I said. My throat had tightened up.

"A stroke knocked him down," the lady continued, as if she'd never paused. "He lived for several hours afterward and kept calling me Bobby. So I was Bobby and he was no longer Ben. How quickly things can change."

She looked at me with those sad eyes. They were a faded green, like cola bottles left in the sun too long. "You know, the bags attached to some of the residents contain the drainage from broken hearts."

"Oh," I said again. My own heart felt cracked. The one word spurred the lady on.

"When I was with Ben on the farm, the

days were three different colors," she said. "Morning was yellow, with sunshine bathing the kitchen in a warm golden light. The endless sky over the fields made noon blue and green, and evening was a soft gray, like a newborn kitten's fur. Now the days pass by in a blur, a shade of beige like calf poop."

I looked at Chris, who didn't seem to be listening. She was taking the lady's blood pressure.

"That's nice," I said, biting my lip.

"No, it's not nice," the lady snapped. "Here I am, an old lady with Brillo pad hair and a face like a road map, growing older all alone in a rest home. I wanted to grow old with Ben on the farm with the different-colored days and the sweet nights. Here in this place, the days are calf poop and the nights are sour pickles. And everything—I mean *everything*—is *blue!* Blue, blue, blue. I hate it."

I figured I'd better not take any more chances on opening my mouth and having the wrong thing spill out. I nodded.

The lady closed her eyes. "Ben's favorite

color was yellow. I was wearing canary-
yellow on the day we met, ice-skating on
Nolt's Pond. My best friend Sara had said
that if you wear yellow, you'll catch a fel-
low. Well, I caught Benjamin Skiles right
there on Nolt's Pond, like a fish in a net."
She cackled and opened her eyes.

"You'd look good in yellow, young lady,
with that strawberry-blonde hair of yours."

Strawberry-blonde. Nobody had ever called
my hair such a beautiful name before. I decided right then and there that this was a
lady I wanted to get to know.

"Thank you," I said, tossing my long and
luxurious strawberry-blonde hair. I couldn't
wait to get me something yellow to wear.

The other residents were dull as dishwater
after Amelia Skiles. The ladies were quiet
and reserved and the two men—Walter
Smucker and Sterling King—were bashful
and rabbity.

At the end of the day—after I'd made
beds, toted water, cleaned bathrooms, and
buttoned hundreds of buttons—I stopped at
Amelia's room to say good-bye. She was

rocking in a chair by the window, staring at the woods surrounding Blue Moon. "Just thought I'd say good-bye before I left," I said.

Amelia squinted. "That's what really made me mad at Ben," she said. "He never said good-bye."

All night, even as I did the dishes, I turned Amelia's words over in my mind. *Ben never said good-bye.* Those words sent an eerie feeling down my spine, and halfway through the supper dishes I figured it out.

Mama never said good-bye, either.

CHAPTER 9

A Letter to Mama

I'd been biding my time for more than four years, just waiting for my mama to come back. Or at least to say good-bye, so I could move on with my life.

As I stood in the kitchen, slathering butter and mayonnaise on white bread for Pa's lunch, I was hit by a brainstorm. Write Mama a letter. There was only one problem. I needed her address and didn't want to come right out and ask Pa for it. We rarely talked about Mama in front of Pa.

I knew that Pa had a metal box in his closet that he called his filing cabinet. In Pa's filing cabinet were all the important papers, like the title to his truck, our birth certificates, and Pa's social security card. I figured that if Pa had Mama's address it would be in there, in that black metal box. I recalled Pa's getting divorce papers from Pittsburgh and shoving them in the box.

When Pa got off the sofa to change the channel (our television didn't come with remote control, like the Shepherds' did), I casually called in to him.

"Hey, Pa," I said, cool as a cucumber. "Do you happen to know where my Sunday school perfect-attendance papers are?"

"Why?" Pa asked.

"Oh, I'd just like to show them to Grace. You know, give her a little incentive to go downstairs to children's church every Sunday." It was a lie, and a lie about church at that, but I hoped God would realize it was for a good cause.

"They're in my black filing cabinet," Pa said. "But don't go messing everything up in there." I didn't see how Pa's closet could possibly get any more messed up than it already was, but I didn't say that.

"Thank you, Pa," I said.

He grunted.

I tiptoed down the hallway, hoping that Grace was too busy with her dolls to notice. Grace was into cutting the hair off her Barbie dolls and using markers to give them three different shades of eye shadow. The result was kind of a punk-rock Barbie sporting a dirty pink ball gown.

"What are you doing in Pa's room?" Grace called from our bed. As I said, that child never missed a trick.

"Looking for something," I said.

"What?"

"My brain. I left it in here." That was one of Pa's sayings.

"Jonathan Shepherd said that when the Lord was passing out brains, you thought He said trains and let Him pass on by," Grace said.

"He did not," I said. "Did he?"

"That's for me to know and you to find

out," Grace taunted. Now that she was five years old, she thought she was big stuff.

I stepped through a mountain of Pa's work clothes and boots, over to his closet. The door on that closet never shut right, and it was hanging crooked. I yanked it open and rooted through piles of Pa's tools and flannel shirts. Finally, I found the filing cabinet in the back right corner, the same spot where I stashed my Wish Books. I suppose everybody hides important things in the back right corners of closets.

I sifted through the papers until I discovered the divorce stuff. And there it was. Ruby L. Musser, 110 Parkside Lane, Pittsburgh, Pennsylvania. Where jobs are plentiful and money grows on trees and mamas don't miss their babies.

After Pa went to bed, I huddled over the kitchen table and wrote until my hand cramped up. Then I read the letter out loud and pretended I was Mama, receiving a letter from my firstborn daughter.

Dear Mama,

I reckon you're as stunned as a cow against an electric fence to be getting a letter from me. About time, wouldn't you say?

How's Pittsburgh? Have you ever gone rafting on the river? Sometimes I dream that you and me and Grace are shooting the rapids and having a good old time. In the dream, I can't see your face, but I can hear you laughing.

There isn't much laughing going on around here. Pa still stonewalls, as you used to say, whenever I try to talk to him about anything that cuts too close to the heart. He's still drinking, and sometimes his eyes are streaked with little red lines like a road map. Did you and the Rainbow man follow a road map to Pittsburgh, or did you just follow your hearts?

After you left, Pa threw away all the clothes you left behind and gave your musical jewelry box to Goodwill. He said that he wanted to get rid of anything that you ever touched. I suppose he forgot that included me and Grace.

I found a locket in your sock drawer, but I can't open it. Pa doesn't know I have it. Sometimes I pretend that if I ever opened the locket, it would bring you back home, like magic. Pa says that trying to hold you on this mountain would be like trapping a lightning bug in a mason jar.

The real reason I'm writing, Mama, is to tell you that I think Pa's time may be running out. A couple of nights ago, he snuck out while Grace and I were in bed, to see Doc Jeffries. I'm afraid that maybe all those cigarettes are catching up to him.

Wouldn't you like to come say good-bye? To Pa and to me and to Grace and to this mountain that held you captive for thirty years? You didn't even say good-bye or turn around for one last look as you flew away with the Rainbow man.

By the way, Aunt Virginia bought a
Rainbow vacuum, but Pa said that he
wouldn't even clean the pigpen with it.
Please write back as soon as possible.

Maizie

P.S. If you come back home, would
you allow me to have my ears pierced?
At my age, pierced ears are important.

CHAPTER 10

Mamaw Blue

"It's terrible when you're old and want to gussy up," Amelia Skiles fussed. "You can't apply makeup with your glasses on, and you can't see with them off, and they give you a headache anyway, if you wear them or not. All your shoes are uncomfortable, and your support stockings fall down around your ankles or get runners. And you can't find the holes for your earrings."

I poked the post of a round pink earring through the tiny hole in Amelia's wrinkled ear. This reminded me of threading a needle. You must have a lot of patience.

"You're lucky to have pierced ears," I said, but Amelia didn't seem to hear me.

"Here I am rusting away in a rest home," she said. "Maybe they should call it 'rust home.' Getting old is the pits."

"Being young isn't always the greatest, either," I muttered.

Amelia looked at me. "What? Speak up, girl."

"I said, 'BEING YOUNG ISN'T ALWAYS A BOWL OF CHERRIES.' Especially if you're sort of in between being young and being grown-up."

"In between, my eye! You're a green apple, Maizie Musser."

That was the first time I'd been called a green apple, but then I'd never known anyone quite like Amelia Skiles. She was the most plainspoken person I'd ever met.

"How long have you had pierced ears?" I asked, working on the other ear.

"Two years. Since Ben died," Amelia said. "I decided that since I had a hole in my heart, I might as well have a couple in my ears."

"My pa says that I already have a hole in the head, so what do I need two in the ears for?" I said.

"What's your ma say?" Amelia asked.

"Nothing," I said. "She's dead." That was two lies in two days, but I wasn't in the mood to explain that my mama ran off with a vacuum cleaner man and couldn't care less about my ears.

"Oh," Amelia said. She didn't say that she was sorry. I guess she felt sorry only for herself.

"Do you like horses?" I asked as I made the bed.

Amelia shrugged. "I can take them or leave them," she said.

"I'm saving my money for a strawberry roan pony," I said. "That's why I got this job."

Amelia yawned and tugged on an earring.

"Do you have any children?" I asked.

"One. But I can't stand him," Amelia said. "His name is Roe, and he's too big for his britches."

Brother Roe! Amelia Skiles was Brother

Roe's mother! I felt like a fool for not con-
necting the names Skiles, but I didn't often
think of him as having a last name. He was
just Brother Roe to me.

"Why can't you stand him?" I asked. I
wasn't about to tell Amelia that I knew her
son and couldn't stand him, either. After all,
you're supposed to love everyone in your
church family.

"Oh, he's got a swelled head." Amelia
waved off my question like a pesky insect.

"Any grandchildren?" I asked. Pa always
said that I asked too many questions and that
curiosity killed the cat.

"What woman in her right mind would
marry my Roe?" Amelia asked.

"I didn't know that a mother could dislike
her own flesh and blood," I said. Maybe that
was why Mama took off. Maybe she despised
Grace and me.

"A mother isn't a saint," Amelia said.
"She's only human."

I repeated Amelia's words every day for
weeks. Whenever I ran out to the mailbox,
all fired up about the possibility of a letter

from Mama, I said it to myself: "A mother isn't a saint. She's only human." And then I wasn't quite so let down when no letter appeared.

Maybe she's busy taking care of the Rainbow man, I thought. *Maybe she's down with the flu. Maybe she broke her hand, the one she writes with. Maybe the postal service went on strike in Pittsburgh.*

After six weeks and still no reply, I thought that maybe she really didn't care. Maybe she couldn't stand me. Maybe she thought I was too big for my britches, having the gall to write a letter after all these years.

When I told Becky about it, she said that Mama probably felt too guilty for what she'd done and that my letter probably made the shame worse. That she was most likely filled with humiliation and regret. That she'd never be able to show her face on this mountain again.

"It would be bold as brass for her to ever come back, Maizie," Becky said. "Just think of all the names she'd be called." Becky sprawled on her pink canopy bed, her head resting on her satin pillowcase. We always had serious discussions on Becky's bed. It was the most private and quiet place in her house. In my home, there was *no* private and quiet place.

"Names?" I asked. The only names I'd ever heard her called were Ruby, Mrs. Musser, and Mama. And Pa used to call her Ruby Lou.

"Oh, you know," Becky said, putting her hand in front of her face and whispering. "Wanton woman, Jezebel, shameless hussy."

I was furious. "Let those who have no sin cast the first stone," I said, repeating something I'd heard Pastor John say.

I lay back on the other pillow. Becky's teddy bear, the one with real pearls for buttons, perched on top of her bed. I picked Pearly up and cradled her in my arms. "I don't even know why we're talking about it, Becky. She's never coming back."

Becky leaned on her elbow and peered at me through her new lavender-tinted glasses. "Why do you say that?" she asked.

"For starters, she would have answered my letter."

"Maybe she never got it. Maybe it was stolen from your mailbox or lost somewhere along the way. Pittsburgh is a long way away, you know."

"Yes, I know," I said. "Also, I found out that there are some mothers who despise their own children."

"Where'd you find that out?" Becky looked upset that I'd learned something somewhere other than from her.

"From that lady at the home that I told you about. Amelia. We have serious discussions and she tells me things like that. Grown-up secrets and stuff that only mothers know."

"You have serious discussions with somebody other than me?" Becky squealed. "I thought we were blood sisters." Five years ago, when Becky and I first became best friends, we pricked our fingers with one of her mother's sewing needles and mingled our blood. That was before we'd heard of AIDS and hepatitis and other dreadful

ailments a person could get from dirty needles.

"We are blood sisters, Becky. But this lady
is different. I can tell her anything because
she doesn't get shocked or excited or mad.
Amelia is kind of a . . . a . . ." I groped for
a term to describe the relationship that I had
with Amelia Skiles. "She's my Mamaw
Blue!" I blurted.

Becky looked puzzled. "She is? She's your
grandmother?"

"Not my real grandmother, silly. Amelia
is kind of my adopted grandmother, the mamaw I always wished I had to talk with when
I'm feeling blue and down in the dumps.
She's somebody who's been around longer
and so she knows more than me . . . or you."
I looked at Becky, and to my surprise she
was smiling.

"Your Mamaw Blue," she said, rolling the
words around on her tongue like a piece of
gum. "I like that. That's great, Maizie. What
does she look like?"

"Well, not like the mamaws in my Wish

Book, but real nice," I said. "Life isn't a Sears catalog, you know."

"I know," Becky said, and hugged me. "I'm glad that your wish for a mamaw came true." She fluffed her frizzy hair.

"Now," Becky said, "wait until you see the new mood shirt that Daddy bought for me. It turns green when I'm happy, black when I'm sad, and orange when I'm worried about something."

Becky hopped from her bed and our serious discussion ended, as I fretted about how to tell Amelia Skiles that she was now my Mamaw Blue.

CHAPTER 11

Digging for a Pony

"Did you ever have a nickname, Amelia?" I asked.

She scrunched up her face and tapped on her head as she thought. "Mealy Worm," she finally said. "A boy in school used to call me that."

"Boys never change," I said. "Would you mind if I gave you a nickname?"

Amelia shrugged. "Go ahead," she said.

I took a deep breath. "Mamaw Blue," I said.

Amelia squinted. "What's a Ma-maw?" she asked.

"It's a word that some of the mountain people use instead of grandmother," I explained. "Down south it's real common."

"But why blue?" she squawked. "I hate blue."

"It popped into my mind because of Blue Moon," I said. "And also because I can talk to you when I'm feeling blue. You're like the grandmother I've always wished for."

Amelia nodded, and a funny look crossed her face. "Mamaw Blue it is," she said. "It's nice to have a granddaughter who's so pretty and smart." Her voice cracked.

Something in Amelia's voice touched me deep inside and I spilled my guts, telling her all about Mama and the Rainbow man and my Wish Books. And about Pa and Grace and how worried I was about Pa's health. And about Aunt Virginia, my Sunday mother. And even how I wrote a letter to my mama but she hasn't answered and I didn't know if she ever would.

I talked a tin ear. Amelia just listened and nodded, never saying a word. When I finally finished, she shook her head. "You've had a lot dumped on your shoulders, Maizie," she said.

I sighed, feeling sorry for myself.

Amelia reached out and took my hand in hers."You're strong enough to carry the burden, Maizie. I see a lot of myself in you." She looked down at our hands. "Ben ran out on me, and your mama ran out on you. Only difference is, Pittsburgh is still on this earth. You're lucky. . . . You still have your mama even though she's not with you. I don't have Ben, except in his Memory Box."

"Memory Box?" I asked.

"I have two Memory Boxes," Amelia said. "One is for Ben, the other is for President John F. Kennedy. The two men I admired and loved more than anything in this world. You want to see Ben's Memory Box?"

I nodded, even though I was scared to death. A Memory Box sounded so personal, and snooping around in one might be like reading somebody's diary or poking around in their drawers. I didn't know what might be found in a Memory Box.

Amelia hobbled over to the bureau and yanked on the bottom drawer. She pulled out a shoe box with the words BEN'S MEMORY BOX scrawled across the lid. "I put everything in here that reminded me of Ben," she said, opening the box. "Pictures, old love letters, his John Deere cap, the wallet I gave him on his last birthday, a scrap of his bathrobe, his wedding ring, a kernel of the silver queen corn he grew, a piece of Wrigley's Spearmint. And I wrote him a letter after he died, telling him how angry I was that he'd left me even though I loved him." Amelia looked at me. "That's what you need to do. Get those feelings out. Let off steam. You'll explode someday if you don't."

I nodded, and she handed me a yellowed old photograph.

"That was Ben on the worst day of our lives. A flood had destroyed all our crops, and I'd just lost a baby girl. But in a Memory Box, you must save both the good and the bad. Even if it hurts to remember, a Memory Box will hold that pain for you."

"Did you ever think of getting another husband?" I asked. "Like maybe Walter Smucker or Sterling King?"

Amelia snorted. "Walter Smucker mucks everything up, and old Sterling is a bit tarnished. Anyway, there's no replacing somebody who's been so important in your life. That's like substituting saccharin for sugar. It's a good imitation, but it could never be the real thing."

"What's in your President Kennedy Memory Box?" I asked.

"The hardcover book I bought, some magazine articles about JFK, a picture of him throwing John-John into the air, a handkerchief I was ironing when the news came over the radio that JFK had been shot. I burned a hole clean through that hankie and told Ben, 'This is what my life will be like without JFK. There will always be a hole, an emptiness.' "

My eyes burned. That was exactly how I'd been feeling since Mama left. Empty.

"JFK was almost as special as my Ben. There will never be another like Ben," Amelia declared. "He was a diamond in a manure pile."

I started to laugh and couldn't stop. Tears streamed down my face and my jaw ached. Amelia just looked at me and said, "You're too young for all this misery. Get it out, be done with it, and go on with your life. You can't look forward to tomorrow and still hold on to yesterday."

She opened another drawer and pulled out a box of apricot-colored stationery, with seashells floating around the edges of the paper. "Write your mama, Maizie," Amelia said. "Everybody deserves a second chance."

I nodded. "You're right. Where would I be without second chances?" I wiped my eyes.

"And now," said Amelia, "how much money do you need for that strawberry roan pony you're always squawking about?"

"I don't know, exactly," I said. "I figure about a thousand bucks, till I get the saddle and all."

"And how much have you made so far?"

I picked at a thread dangling from the hem

of my uniform. "Six hundred dollars and twenty-three cents," I said. "But I gave three hundred to my pa to help pay off the electric bill."

Amelia frowned. "So you have three hundred dollars and twenty-three cents?"

"Not exactly," I said. "I bought a doll for Grace and a yellow dress for myself, to wear to church."

"Exactly how much money do you have, Maizie?" Amelia lowered herself shakily into the rocking chair.

I took a deep breath. "Two hundred and sixty dollars and one cent," I said.

The rocking chair squeaked, and Amelia stared out the window. The blue curtains flapped in the breeze. "Do you realize that summer is halfway over?" she asked.

I nodded. "I'll get the money somehow," I said. "That strawberry roan is my heart's desire."

Amelia turned with a sly grin. "Meet me on the front porch at sundown," she said. "Bring some helping hands and somebody to drive a car. We'll get you some money."

At eight o'clock, Amelia was swaying on the porch swing, the heels of her pink shoes dragging across the blue boards. She scrutinized Aunt Virginia's little red car as we zoomed into the driveway. "Lost half your car!" she shouted as Grace, Aunt Virginia, and I trudged up the steps.

"It's a convertible, sugar," Aunt Virginia said. "The top goes up and down."

"Just like Maizie's moods," Amelia said, and cackled.

"How old are you?" Grace asked, gawking at Amelia.

Amelia ignored Grace and heaved herself off the swing. "Let's go," she said. "We've got money to earn."

We all squeezed into Dixie, which is what Aunt Virginia called her car. "Down Spooky Nook, make a left, up Mountain, and across Raccoon Hill. First farm on the right," Amelia said.

"Where are we going?" asked Grace. She bounced on the seat, which was covered with a soft material Aunt Virginia called kitten leather.

"Strawberry roan hunting," Amelia said.

Grace crinkled her forehead. "But we don't have any guns," she said.

"Don't need guns, just shovels," said Amelia.

"We're going to dig a pony out of the ground?" Grace asked.

"Something like that," said Amelia as we bounced along the stone lane toward the farmhouse. "Good. Roe's gone to work. Leaves every night at sundown for that high-falutin health-food store down in the valley."

"Amelia, what are we doing?" I asked. I was a bit shy about calling her Mamaw Blue, especially in front of Grace and Aunt Virginia. I never was one for wearing my heart on my sleeve.

"Digging!" Amelia replied. She swung open the car door and teetered across the yard. "I've been wanting to do this for two years," she said, rubbing her hands together.

Amelia lifted the latch on a rotting barn door and disappeared inside. A few minutes later, she came through the open door, lugging two shovels, a hoe, and a spade. There was a smudge on her silky dress.

"Why'd you get all dressed up just to dig?" asked Grace. "Who lives here?"

"My son," Amelia said, sideswiping Grace's first question. She handed me a rusty shovel. "Don't just stand there with your mouths hanging open," she said. "Get digging!"

Aunt Virginia and I looked at each other. "What are we digging for?" she whispered.

"Coffee cans," I said. "Her husband buried them all over the yard, filled with cash."

"Don't just stand there!" Aunt Virginia hollered. "Get digging!" She prissily picked up the spade and poked at the dirt. "I do declare I'll have a conniption if I bust a fingernail," she muttered.

Grace grabbed the hoe, which was taller than she, and chopped at the ground. "I'm digging for a roan pony," she sang.

"You may keep any money you find," Amelia said as Grace kneeled down and hoisted a tin can from the soil.

"Twenty dollars," I said, opening the plastic lid and peering inside the dusty can. All of a sudden, there was a rumble and the yard was flooded with light.

"Mother!" bellowed Brother Roe. "What in the world are you doing?"

Amelia drew herself up. "What in the world are *you* doing, coming home from work so early?" she demanded, her voice dripping with motherly authority.

"I came home sick," Brother Roe said meekly, rubbing his throat. In the light of the full moon, I could see that his pants were clinging to his ankles.

Aunt Virginia sashayed across the yard and daintily extended her ringed fingers for a handshake. "Nice to meet you, Mr. Skiles," she drawled. "I've heard so much about you."

"Good or bad?" Brother Roe stammered.

"Good as gold," Aunt Virginia said, taking his arm. "You need to get yourself a cup of steaming catnip tea," she purred. "Fixes whatever ails you."

"Aunt Virginia could charm the stripe off

a polecat," I whispered to Amelia as we watched the two of them head for the kitchen of the farmhouse.

Grace jumped up and hugged Amelia around the waist. "Thank you for the money, Mealy," she said.

Amelia gazed at Grace, her heels sinking into the mushy earth. "Call me Mamaw Blue," she said.

Grace grinned, and her dimple darted across her left cheek. "Mamaw Blue," she said. "What can I buy with twenty dollars?"

CHAPTER 12

Hard Work
Never Hurt Anyone

Grace and I decided to spend the money on some paint for the barn. At least, *I* decided and Grace agreed, after some persuasion on my part. I had to promise her a new puppy to live in the barn, to seal the deal.

"Will it have a white spot on its belly like Luther?" she asked as I dipped the paintbrush in the can of Flaming Rose. It had been a toss-up between Flaming Rose, Cheery Cherry, Blazing Brick, Glowing Geranium, and Ruby Russet Red. I was seeing red for hours after our visit to Pete's Paint Point. We gazed at all those different shades until my eyes blurred and the whole *world* looked red.

"If it's a beagle, it'll probably have some white spots," I replied. I had drops of Flaming Rose on my leg.

"How do you know it'll be a beagle?" Grace trailed a twig through the paint and colored the grass.

"Don't waste the paint, Grace," I said. "Think of it as liquid gold, at the price we had to pay." Twenty dollars had bought only two gallons of Pete's Econo-Paint, and I was praying that would be enough for one coat.

Grace tossed the twig into the air and red paint drizzled on her nose. "How do you know it'll be a beagle?" she asked again.

"Because Gertrude's dog had another litter," I said. "I'm planning to go talk to Gertrude after supper."

"To ask her for a puppy?" Grace scratched her nose and smeared the paint.

"To ask her for a puppy and a job," I said. I dipped the brush in the can and shook it, trying to keep the amount thin.

"A job?" asked Grace. "You already have a job."

"I need another one if I'm going to earn a strawberry roan by the end of the summer," I said. "I need about a thousand dollars, and there are only six more weeks of summer. That means about six hundred more dollars from Blue Moon."

Grace's eyes got as round as the paint can. "That's a lot of money," she said.

"Yes, it is," I agreed. "But not enough. So I'm planning to ask Gertrude if I can work her truck patch for her." Gertrude had a big truck patch and a bad back, so she couldn't bend over to weed the tomatoes or pick peas.

"Do you need to wear a uniform for that, like at Blue Moon?" Grace asked.

I shook my head and slowly stroked the paintbrush across the oak boards. "Don't touch this, Grace," I said, standing back to admire my handiwork.

Grace was rolling in the grass. "Too bad we didn't dig up more money before Brother Roe came home and made us stop," she said, grubbing around in the garden dirt. "Mamaw Blue says there's lots of money buried there."

"The twenty dollars you found bought this paint," I said.

"And part of my paycheck went for the paintbrush and the gas for the truck," Pa said. He had sneaked up behind me. "Pete's Paint Point isn't just a stone's throw away, you know."

"I know," I said, turning around and smiling. "Thank you, Pa."

He just grunted and headed back toward the trailer. As he opened the door, he called, "You're doing a fine job, Maizie."

"Thank you, Pa," I said again. Our best hen, Harriet, clucked at my feet. Harriet laid beautiful brown eggs speckled with maroon, with a red spot inside. The drops of Flaming Rose reminded me of Harriet's eggs. I was seeing red everywhere, it seemed.

"Let me paint, Maizie," Grace begged.

I handed her the paintbrush. "Slowly and carefully," I instructed, guiding her hand to the wood. She swatted the brush across the board and flecks of Flaming Rose splattered in her hair. "My turn," I said, taking back the brush.

"Is Mama going to answer your letter, Maizie?"

I sighed. "I really don't know, Grace. I don't know everything, you know."

"Do you wish she'd answer your letter?"

"Of course I wish she would, Grace. But wishing doesn't make it so."

Grace frowned. "Jonathan Shepherd says that if you make a wish on your birthday and close your eyes and blow out all the candles on your birthday cake, your wish will come true."

"That's malarkey, Grace. If that were so, then everybody would have everything they ever wanted. Nobody would have to work."

"Or have Wish Books," Grace said.

I painted in silence for a few minutes as Grace and Wooly Girl watched. The only sounds were Mrs. Porkenbean snuffling in the pigpen and Wooly Girl yanking grass from the ground.

"Nice work, Maizie." Mr. Flynn's deep

voice boomed across the yard. He came to pick up the rent check every month.

I smiled. "I'm fixing to get me a strawberry roan," I said.

Mr. Flynn was befuddled. "A strawberry roam?" he asked. "Is that a strawberry plant that roams from the garden into the barn, like a creeping vine?" He stroked his handlebar mustache.

Grace giggled. "People who live in the city don't know anything, do they, Maizie?"

"Shush, Grace," I said.

"A strawberry roan is a pony," I explained to Mr. Flynn. "It has a dark coat dappled with pink."

Mr. Flynn scowled. "You're not planning on adding another animal to this menagerie, are you?"

"We're getting two more animals," Grace said. "A roan pony and a new dog." She smiled sweetly at Mr. Flynn and asked, "What's a men . . . whatever?"

I stared at Mr. Flynn. "A menagerie is a collection of wild animals for people to gawk at, Grace. And that's not what we have here."

Mr. Flynn shoved his hands in his pockets and rattled his change. "Sorry, Maizie," he said. "No more animals." He turned on his shiny heel and headed for the trailer.

"Mr. Flynn!" I cried. "I've been working hard for this pony." I blew a strand of hair from my eyes.

"Hard work never hurt anyone," he called without turning.

"Pa says that *you* don't have to work because we give you a paycheck every month," Grace said. "Right, Maizie?" Grace was hovering by my side.

"Mind your tongue, Grace," I hissed. "How about if I built an addition onto the barn?" I called to Mr. Flynn.

"Sorry, Maizie," he said as he rapped on the back door. "No more animals."

"Not even a little puppy?" Grace whimpered. "Our other dog died."

Mr. Flynn turned to look at Grace. "I suppose one puppy wouldn't hurt anything," he said.

"Ask him about the pony," I whispered from the side of my mouth.

"May we get a roan pony?" Grace asked, squeezing my leg. "Please?"

"Sorry, Maizie." Mr. Flynn disappeared into the trailer, taking with him my hopes and dreams.

"I used to think he was nice," I muttered. "Shows how much I know." I plunged the paintbrush into the can of Flaming Rose and whacked it across the wood for a good five minutes.

"They say that redheads have hot tempers," Mr. Flynn said as he came out of the trailer and strode across the yard. He smiled. "What do you think, Maizie?"

"I reckon they're right," I said, gritting my teeth and slapping paint onto the barn.

"You've got paint splattered above your eyes," Mr. Flynn said, squinting in the sunlight. "You'll be seeing red."

"I already am," I snapped, swiping furiously at my eyes. "I already am, Mr. Flynn."

Mr. Flynn shrugged. "I really am sorry, Maizie. You'll understand someday." He hopped into his shimmery gray car, gunned the engine, and roared from the driveway.

"No, I won't, Mr. Flynn," I said as I watched the exhaust fumes float away like an evaporated wish. "There are some things in this world I'll never understand."

I dipped the paintbrush into the last of the paint and painstakingly stroked it across the one remaining faded barn board, transforming it into something new and shiny and beautiful. Like magic.

Where was *my* magic? Was it inside that silver heart-shaped locket Mama left behind? Or was it within me?

CHAPTER 13

Tough Like Lace

"I'll take the runt of the litter," I said, pointing to the scrawny pup scrambling across Gertrude's linoleum floor.

Gertrude shoved her thick glasses up on her nose. "Why would you want the runt?" she asked. "Why not one of the strong ones?"

I knelt down and patted the beagle's little head. "Because they don't need anybody," I said.

The teakettle whistled, and Gertrude shuffled across the floor. "You're staying for some meadow tea," she said. It was more a command than a question, so I sat on a wobbly chair that was patched with duct tape.

"Do you need help with your garden, by any chance?" I asked.

Gertrude laughed, a sound like a rumble of thunder rolling from her throat. "I sure do, honey. I need help with everything."

I took a deep breath. Grace was right. Gertrude's house really did smell like cabbage. "I'll work your truck patch for ten dollars a week," I said. "I grow the biggest tomatoes on the mountain. Pa says I have a green thumb."

Gertrude nodded and placed a cup of tea before me. "You've got yourself a deal, Maizie." She reached out and touched my hair. "A green thumb and red hair," she said.

"Not red," I said. "Strawberry-blonde." Pa used to say that my hair put him in mind of strained rhubarb. It's funny how a few words can change the way you feel about yourself. When Amelia said those words— *strawberry blonde*—my whole perception of myself started to sparkle.

Gertrude plodded to the other side of the table and looked at me. "You know, Maizie, you're looking more and more like your mama. I recall Ruby Lou having that same determined look in her eyes. You're going to get anything you set your sights on."

I sighed. The puppy I'd chosen flopped at my feet, a bag of bones hitting the faded gold linoleum.

"I always said that your mama would be just like that wild hound we had before Harvey died. The one with the ornery streak, that kept running away and then finding its way home. Some day Ruby Lou will find her way right back to this mountain, where she belongs." Gertrude slapped her large hand on the table.

"What's the puppy's name?" I hated it when Gertrude got on the subject of Mama.

"Didn't give her one." Gertrude eased herself into a chair and slurped her tea. "Ran out of names years ago, after having nine young'uns." She patted her stomach, protruding inside her plaid dress.

I petted the pup, who rolled over onto her back. There was a spidery white design on her stomach. It reminded me of the latticework around Gertrude's big front porch. "I think I'll call her Lacy," I said.

"Lazy is a fine name," Gertrude said. "Especially if she's anything like her mother, Lucy Fay, or her late half brother Luther."

"Not *Lazy*," I said. "Lacy. Like your doilies." I pointed to the fancy white mats decorating Gertrude's windowsills.

"But lace is so flimsy," Gertrude said. "That pup is feeble enough without such a namby-pamby name."

I sipped my tea. "Lace is tougher than it looks," I said. "Just like me."

Gertrude goggled at me. "Tough you are, Maizie Musser. When that mama of yours went gallivanting off across the state, you took on a burden too strong for those gangly little arms of yours. Why, you took care of Grace and your pa better than most grown women would have! Never in my life—"

"Gertrude," I interrupted, "have you ever had horses in that barn?" I pointed through the window at the slumping gray structure that slouched behind the house.

" 'Course we had horses!" Gertrude

paused to cough. "Back in my day, I could ride a horse like nobody's business. I always say, there ain't nothin' like a wild stallion to calm the nerves." She pushed up her glasses and cleared her throat.

"Gertrude," I said, "if I got myself a horse, how much would you charge to let me board it in your barn?"

Gertrude bowed her head and thought for a minute. I stared at her thin gray hair until she looked up and said, "Ten dollars a week. If you help in the garden, I'll keep your horse."

"Thank you, Gertrude," I said.

"Save your thanks for a spell," Gertrude said. "I've got a gift for you." She trudged over to a huge hutch squatting in a corner and rummaged through a drawer.

"Here it is," she huffed, tossing me a black velvet hair bow glittering with shiny sequins. "Your mama left it here, back before she took leave of her senses."

"Thank you, Gertrude," I said again. I stroked the silky velvet and wondered if I'd ever have occasion to wear anything so fancy.

CHAPTER 14

Flashes

"Hold still, Grace. I want to capture this moment in pencil for Mama." I was sketching Grace and Lacy wrestling in the yard. The only problem was that they didn't know how to wrestle in slow motion.

"I don't know how to hold still, Maizie," Grace said. "How can I hold still when Lacy is licking my face?"

"Just try," I said. "I only have one pigtail to go." Mama would be sorry she left when she saw how pretty Grace had become.

"Are you sending this with the letter?" Grace asked, eyeing the picture over my shoulder.

I nodded, folding the sketch in half and sticking it into the envelope.

"Read me the letter, Maizie." Grace plopped on the ground, clutching poor Lacy on her lap. Grace has quite a grip, like me.

"Okay." I sighed and pulled the letter from the envelope. I'd used the apricot stationery that Mamaw Blue had given me.

"Dear Mama," I read. "Lately I've been remembering things about you, like how you used to sing along with love songs on the radio and dance with the mop. I remember that you wrecked your car once and that you used to give me thumbs-up when you kissed me good night. I remember your belly all big with Grace.

"When I worked up the nerve to tell Pa some of the things I was remembering, he just grunted and shook his head. Then he said that your mind was affected by all the soap operas you used to watch and that he'd better not ever catch me watching the soaps. He said soaps dirty the mind.

"The seventeen-year locusts are here, making a racket day and night. Are there locusts in Pittsburgh? Pa says that you'll probably be like the locusts and maybe show up every seventeen years or so. I pray that he's wrong, because I'll be too old to need a mama by then.

"Pa says I should dare you to come back, because you never were one to pass up a dare. So I dare you, Mama. I double-dare you to come back to the Welsh Mountain, where you belong.

"Maizie."

When I finished, Grace stared at the ground for a moment. Then she asked, "How big was Mama's belly with me?"

I wrestled Grace and Lacy to the ground and said, "Too big, Grace. Too big for a scrawny little runt like you."

After I sent that second letter, I started having memory flashes. I'd be doing some common, everyday chore like hanging out laundry or scrubbing the floor when suddenly I'd be flooded with pictures from the past. It was as if the Niagara Falls of memories crashed down on my head.

One day I was frying some eggs for Grace

when I remembered how Mama used to make dippy eggs for me and decorate the yellow part with a ketchup face.

Another time I remembered that she used a yardstick to flush the toilet, standing way back so that she wouldn't inhale any germs. "Every time you flush a toilet, millions of germs spew into the air," she said. "With all the germs in the world, it's a wonder anybody is still alive."

Maybe she moved to Pittsburgh because there are no germs there.

About the time I started having memory flashes, Pa started having welder's flashes. He'd be sitting staring into space when all of a sudden there'd be tears pouring down his face.

"What's wrong, Pa?" I asked the first time it happened. Seeing Pa cry scared me, like watching a giant building fall to the ground in shambles.

"Nothing," he said, swiping at the tears. "Welder's flash, that's all."

"What's that?" I asked.

"It happens all the time. A welder accidentally looks at the arc, maybe because his helmet didn't come down fast enough or because he forgot his safety glasses. That night, he's bound to get a welder's flash from looking at the bright light. It's like looking at an eclipse of the sun without eye protection."

Pa wouldn't look at me, and he seemed to be talking faster than usual. Also, he was cracking his knuckles. Pa always cracks his knuckles when he's fibbing.

"Pa, you've been welding for more years than I've been alive. Don't tell me that you forgot your glasses or didn't put your helmet down fast enough."

"I've been awful forgetful lately, Maizie. I'd forget my fool head if it wasn't attached." He tried to laugh, but it came out more like a sigh.

"What's it feel like?" I asked. "Welder's flash, I mean."

"Like somebody's stabbing my eyes out," he said. "Sharp knives in the eyes." His eyes were all red, like on Sunday mornings.

"Is there anything you can do for it?" I asked. "How about eyedrops or ice or tea bags?" I knew all kinds of cures for sore eyes.

"Just time, Maizie," he said, blowing his nose. "It just takes time."

I soon noticed that Pa's welder's flashes always happened right after I'd been hit by a memory flash. That was how I figured out that Pa was still upset by any mention of Mama.

I decided to test my theory of Memory Flash Equals Welder's Flash by showing Pa the locket I'd been hiding all these years. It was tucked away in the back corner of our closet, beneath Grace's outgrown clothes.

"Pa, I have something to show you," I said one night after supper. "Now don't be mad, but I've kept something secret from you for a long time."

"What's that? Your common sense?" Pa asked, chewing on a toothpick.

"Don't be funny, Pa. This is serious," I said, and went to the bedroom to root through Grace's clothes. Most of them were ruined anyway, because Grace was so active, but for some reason I just couldn't bear to throw them away.

"I found this in Mama's sock drawer after she left," I said, handing him the silver heart locket. "I've never been able to pry it open."

Pa seemed to hold his breath, then he rubbed his eyes. Then he got out his pocket-knife and jimmied open the heart. What was inside made us both catch our breath: a picture of all of us together: Mama, Pa, Grace, and me. Grace was about eight months old, so it must have been taken a few months before The Leaving.

Mama was holding Grace, Pa had his arm around my shoulder, and we were all smiling into the camera. Mama was wearing a yellow dress with pearls, Grace was in a frilly pink thing with a bow stuck on her hairless head, I was in a horrendous shade of grape-purple, and Pa's hair was slicked and shiny.

"She looked good in yellow, didn't she, Pa?"

Pa didn't say anything. He walked over to the sofa and sat down, and within seconds he was hit by a severe case of welder's flash. That's when I knew for sure that Pa fibbed about his flashes. They weren't like a stab in the eyes; they were like a stab in the heart.

After that, I kept my memory flashes to myself, and Pa's welder's flashes cleared up. Like he said, it just takes time.

CHAPTER 15

Amazing Grace

It was eight o'clock on a Saturday night and Pa was passed out on the sofa. Grace was working on the Mama Wish Book, and I was counting my money.

"I'd better get a third job," I said out loud to myself. "At this rate, I might as well give up on that strawberry roan." But deep inside I knew that I'd never give up. I'd work a night job if I had to, and between moonlighting and moonstriping, the pony I dreamed of would become a reality. I could see it clear as crystal in my mind's eye: me sitting on a fine leather saddle, the strawberry roan pony and my strawberry-blonde hair gleaming like jewels in the sunlight. I've often heard that if you picture something hard enough, it will come true. Well, I sure was picturing that magnificent strawberry roan pony.

"Do you like this mama, Maizie?" Grace asked, holding up a glossy blonde in a black leather miniskirt.

"I like her cowboy boots," I said. She was strutting across the page in pointy-toed boots with tassels.

"But do you like her?" Grace reached for the glue and squirted a glob onto the back of the picture.

"Not really. She looks like she couldn't love anybody but herself."

"I like her," Grace said, pasting the blonde into the Wish Book. "She's pretty, like our mama used to be."

"Like our mama probably still is," I said.

"Do you think I'll look like her when I'm a mama?" Grace asked. A line creased the fine white skin on her forehead.

"I think you'll act like her," I said, and Grace beamed. She didn't know that wasn't necessarily a compliment.

"Mrs. Shepherd looks sickly without her makeup," Grace said. "She looks like a raccoon."

"What matters is the soul within," I said. I didn't believe Grace, though. Mrs. Shepherd was beautiful.

"Jonathan Shepherd says bad words when his mama isn't listening," Grace said. "And he belches songs, instead of singing them." She grinned wickedly and twirled the scissors.

"He does not," I said. "Does he?"

"He told me that he hates girls with red hair and skinny white legs," Grace said, flipping through the Sears catalog.

I ignored her and tossed my Blue Moon uniform into the sink to soak.

"Want to help with the Baby Brother Wish Book, Maizie?" Grace asked. She was standing on the kitchen chair.

"No, I do not, and sit down," I said, running cold water over my uniform and splashing some on my face. August is the worst month to live in a twelve-by-sixty-foot trailer with no air-conditioning and half the screens missing.

Suddenly, a scream cut through the muggy heat like a cold silver knife. The sound sliced every nerve in my body, and when I could bear to look at Grace, she was on the floor, curled up tight with her hand pressed to her face. Blood was everywhere.

"I told you to sit down," I said, and the words floated slowly through the kitchen, as if in a dream. I grabbed Grace's hand and yanked it away from her face. She wailed and smacked her hand flat against her left eye.

I snatched the sopping uniform from the sink and sloshed it into Grace's free hand. "Hold this against your eye," I said, kicking the scissors across the floor.

"Pa!" I yelled.

Pa was still out cold.

I bolted into the living room and jerked Pa's keys from his pocket, then gathered Grace into my arms. "Where are we going?" she whined, dripping water and blood all over me. "What are you doing?"

"I'm driving you to Blue Moon, to get help." I headed for the door.

"Pa's going to kill you," Grace gasped between sobs.

Now, I knew it was illegal for a not-quite-thirteen-year-old to drive. But I figured it would be a worse crime to allow my little sister to lose an eye from being stabbed by a scissors while falling off a chair. Or for my pa to drive while under the influence.

So I lugged Grace to the truck and took off across the mountain, toward Blue Moon.

"Don't you know what you're doing, Maizie?" Grace cried as I ground the gears from first into second. She was huddled in the middle of the seat.

I took a deep breath. "Of course I know what I'm doing, Grace. Don't I always?" My left foot groped for the clutch.

I turned onto Spooky Nook Road a little too fast, and Grace nearly fell on the floor. Then I had to downshift, and next thing you know, the truck stalled.

"Why are we stopping on this road?" Grace whispered. "I hate Spooky Nook

Road." An owl hooted somewhere in the darkness, and Grace began to wail.

"Calm down, Grace. Everything will be just fine." When I turned the key, the truck sputtered and shook, then died. Shaking, I pumped the gas pedal and turned the key again. Nothing.

Remembering what Pa always did in such a situation, I moved the gearshift into the neutral position.

"What are you doing, Maizie?" Grace howled as I opened my door.

"Giving the truck a little push," I said. "Stay right where you are, Grace. Everything will be just fine."

I hopped out and, with one hand steering the wheel, pushed the truck slowly down Spooky Nook Road. Something furry brushed my leg, and I screamed. In the yellowish glow of the headlights, I saw a black critter streaked with a flash of white. Then I smelled it . . . skunk.

"You smell bad, Maizie," Grace said when I jumped back into the coasting truck and shifted into second while pumping the gas pedal. Like magic, the truck spluttered to life and we were on our way.

"I'm driving Pa's truck," I said, clutching the wheel. "I'm actually driving Pa's truck." My heart pounded like hail on the trailer roof.

"When will we be there, Maizie?" Grace asked in the high whiny voice that grates on my nerves. "How far?" Her head pushed hard against my leg.

"Soon, Grace. Soon."

I could see Blue Moon, shining blue and white in the night like a beacon. "We're so close now," I said to Grace, "if it were a snake, it'd bite us."

I glanced down at Grace, and when I looked up, something leaped from the woods into the path of the headlights. All I saw were gleaming eyes and brown hair and huge branchlike antlers soaring into the sky. I shrieked and swerved to avoid hitting the deer and . . .

CRASH!

The front end of the truck smashed against one of the tall trees lining Blue Moon's yard.

"Pa's really going to kill you now," Grace breathed as the truck backfired like a shot in the night.

Almost sick on the scent of skunk and gasoline fumes, I hauled Grace from the truck and sprinted across the yard with her. "Ssshhh, Grace," I whispered as I lugged her, bawling and bleeding, into Blue Moon.

Chris Sunrise was leaning on the front desk, scribbling on a blue notepad. Her black braid hung down her back like an exclamation point. She whipped around and said, "Maizie! What on earth!"

"Chris." My voice cracked. "Chris, would you take a look at my sister's eye? She poked herself." The pent-up emotions sizzled through my body, and I sunk into a blue vinyl chair, allowing Chris to take Grace from my arms.

"I didn't poke myself." Grace's shrill voice drifted back to me from the infirmary. "The dumb scissors poked me when I fell."

Finally, they came out. "She has a surface laceration of the upper left eyelid," Chris said. "I fixed her up with an eyepatch and some medication."

"Have it taken from my next paycheck," I said, sighing. There went a chunk of my strawberry roan fund.

"I look like a pirate," Grace said, examining her reflection in a mirror above the desk.

"You look like a pain in my neck," I said, but couldn't resist hugging her just a mite as Chris handed her over.

"Everything in this place is blue," Grace complained, giving the nursing home a one-eyed once-over. "Even that lady's hair." She pointed to a resident hobbling across the lobby.

"Let's get out of here," I said, releasing the wriggling Grace from my arms.

"But you wrecked the truck," Grace said loudly. The blue-haired lady stared.

"Shush, Grace," I said. "Does anybody know how to put a pickup truck in reverse?"

"You drove here?" Chris's dark eyes were liquid and shimmery in the fluorescent light, like two cups of black coffee.

I shrugged. "No other choice."

Grace shimmied around on the shiny blue floor. "She got sprayed by a skunk and hit a tree and almost hit a deer." She sang the words to a tune that sounded suspiciously like "Amazing Grace." "Was blind, but now I see," she concluded, touching the eyepatch with a grubby finger.

Chris smiled. "I'll drive you home," she said.

Later, with Chris at the wheel behind the wrecked hood, Grace said, "Know what would happen if I had patches on both eyes, Maizie?"

"What?" I asked, staring straight ahead at our living room light glaring through the threadbare curtains. I wondered what Chris would think of our home. And of our pa, out like a light on our saggy green sofa and smelling of firewater.

"If I had patches on both eyes, I wouldn't have to look at Jonathan Shepherd. He picks his nose."

"He does not!" I said, blushing and glancing at Chris Sunrise, who downshifted confidently and parked the truck. "Does he?"

CHAPTER 16

Sunrise's Savings

Pa sat up, bleary-eyed and stubble-chinned. "What stinks?" he asked, rubbing his eyes.

"Maizie. She got sprayed by a skunk while she was pushing your truck, before we hit the tree." Grace announced all this in an irritatingly proud voice.

"What?" Pa glared at me, and that one word was like a smack in the face.

"It's a long story, Pa," I said. "You see, Grace was standing on the chair with the scissors even though I told her to sit down, and next thing you know, she darn near poked her eye out. So I had to drive her to Blue Moon for help." I bit my fingernail.

"You did *what?*" Pa stuck a cigarette in his mouth and strode out to the stove.

"I really can't stand when you do that, Pa," I muttered as he held the cigarette to the gas flame.

"Smoking is the worst thing you can do for your health, Mr. Musser," Chris said. "Coats your lungs with tar." She flashed her dazzling grin at Pa.

"And who are you?" asked Pa. "The surgeon general?" He blew a gray cloud into the air.

Chris smiled again. "My name is Chris Sunrise," she said. "I work with Maizie, over at Blue Moon."

A smile tugged at Pa's mouth. "Jake Musser," he said, shaking Chris's hand. "Sunrise isn't a common name on this mountain."

"My father was a Navajo Indian," she said, stepping out of the path of Pa's smoke.

Pa sat down at the kitchen table. "Now," he said, taking a deep breath and letting it out slowly, "let's hear it." He looked at me.

"To make a long story short, I wrecked your truck, Pa," I said. I fiddled with Mama's locket, which I was now wearing around my neck. "I'll pay for the repairs."

Grace climbed up on Pa's lap. "She'll never get her roan pony now, will she, Pa?"

Pa stood and poured himself a cup of coffee. He always did that to try to sober himself up. "And where did you get a driver's license, Maizie? Down at Charlie's Cut Rate?"

I sat down and stared at the red and white checked oilcloth. Chris sat across from me. "Aunt Virginia taught me to drive your truck," I said. "She said that I should know how to get from here to there, in case I ever had an emergency when you were drinking."

Pa just shook his head.

"I was almost blind, Pa," Grace said, looking up at him with one blue eye.

Pa sat down and closed his eyes. "Guess I haven't been what I should have been," he said in a low, blurred voice.

I reached across the table to touch his shoulder. "Should-have-beens don't count, Pa," I said. Lacy skittered on the floor, which was still slippery with a pool of water from my drippy uniform.

Pa opened his bloodshot eyes and looked at me, then at Grace. "No more drinking," he said quietly. "Doesn't chase the week away anyway."

I blinked back tears. "Thank you, Pa," I said. "I've been waiting for you to say that for a long time."

"No more smoking, either?" Grace asked, clinging to Pa's neck.

Pa grunted. "One thing at a time, Grace," he said. "One thing at a time." He ran a hand through his rumpled hair. "How bad is the truck?"

I sighed. "Pretty bad. Couple of hundred dollars anyway."

"She'll never get a roan pony," Grace said again.

I traced a square on the oilcloth. "Shush, Grace," I said. "When I put my mind to something, I do it. I'll find a way." I looked at her with (as Gertrude said) "determined eyes."

Chris cleared her throat.

I'd almost forgotten she was there.

"A roan pony?" she asked. "Did you ever hear of a strawberry roan?"

I laughed. "Did I ever hear of it? I *dream* about it."

"She wishes for it," Grace said. "Just like she wishes for a mama."

There was an embarrassed silence, and then Chris said, "If you can come up with about four hundred dollars, I can come up with a strawberry roan."

My heart leaped like a bucking bronco. "I've got it," I said.

"Don't forget about my truck," Pa said. "I can't get to work without a truck."

"Your truck will be fixed, Pa," I said.

"And your part of the electric bill is coming up again," he said.

"I *know*, Pa," I replied, annoyed.

"And school will be starting up again in a couple of weeks," Pa said, running his fingers through his hair.

"I *know*, Pa," I said again.

Pa slurped his coffee as moths batted at

the screen windows. "School's more important than some pink pony," Pa said, sloshing some coffee onto the oilcloth as he put down his cup. "I always say, education is the ticket to a better place."

I set my jaw. "I'll have the money," I said, my words slow and firm.

"And what about Flynn?" Pa asked. "He said no more animals."

"I told you, Pa," I said. "Gertrude will let me board a pony in her barn in exchange for the work I'm doing in her truck patch."

"That barn is a mess," Pa grumbled. "Needs a good cleaning."

"I'll do it," I said.

"And where's the money for pony feed coming from?" Pa asked, taking another sip of coffee.

"I'll get a part-time job after school," I said, shrugging. "And on weekends."

"I'm warning you, Maizie," Pa said, looking at me with his bloodshot eyes. "This durnfool pink pony best not take away from your schoolwork. Your grades fall . . . the pony goes. Deal?"

"Deal," I said, grinning. I looked at Chris. "When can I get the pony?"

"Sometime in early September, when my mother makes the trip from Texas," Chris said.

"It's your mother's horse?" I asked.

Chris nodded. "One of them. Donna Texas is getting old and can't skedaddle like she used to. She needs lots of patience and love."

"I've got lots of both," I said quickly.

"I know," Chris said. "You've got more patience with the Blue Moon residents than any moonstriper I've ever known."

I looked proudly at Pa. "I do have a lot of patience," I said. "Patience is a virtue."

Grace had disappeared, and now she came tripping into the room. "Here's Maizie's Horse Wish Book," she said, slapping the book in front of Chris. "Here's the roan pony she wants."

Chris looked at the picture on the cover. "Donna Texas isn't quite this fantastic," she said.

I smiled. "That's okay," I said. "Real life isn't like a Wish Book."

"But you have our real mama in our Wish Book," Grace said.

There was an awkward silence, and then I changed the subject. I'd never told Chris about our mama. "After Luther died, I didn't know if I wanted to love any creature that much again," I said, picking my words from out of the blue. "Even a strawberry roan." That thought had never really occurred to me before that moment, and I surprised myself with such a statement.

Chris nodded and touched my hand. "My father used to have a saying about that. Joe Sunrise had sayings about everything. He called them Sunrise's Sayings." She smiled. "Let's see. . . . He used to say something about love is here and gone, like the stars that fall, but better to have loved and lost than never to have loved at all."

Pa grunted.

"What did he say about doll babies with short hair?" Grace asked from the floor, where she sat snipping at her Barbie's hair.

"Grace!" I said. "Put those scissors away!"

Chris took the scissors from Grace. "He didn't have a saying about dolls," she said. "But here was his favorite: May you walk in beauty, and may the rainbow touch your shoulder."

We were all quiet for a minute. Then Pa sniffed and said, "May the tomato juice touch Maizie's shoulder. She reeks of skunk."

Everybody laughed, and I noticed that even Lacy seemed to be smiling. I reached down and patted her head as I wondered if Pa really would keep his promise of no more drinking.

CHAPTER 17

A Virus of the Heart

"How do you know if you're really in love?" I asked Aunt Virginia the next day. She was going to church with us, to see Grace be an angel in the children's church annual play.

Aunt Virginia stroked smoky mascara across her eyelashes, her mouth open. "Well, sugar," she said when she was finished, "if your head pounds, your knees shake, and your heart turns to mush, that's it. Love."

"That sounds like the flu," I said, sniffing my arm to see if all those tomato-juice baths had worked.

"A virus of the heart," Aunt Virginia

agreed. "It's easy to catch and awful hard to shake off."

"Are you in love with Brother Roe?" Grace asked, squirming into her glittery white angel costume. It had taken me three hours to sew that gown.

Aunt Virginia laughed. "No, child, I'm not in love with Roe." She brushed Metallic Mauve fingernail polish across her long pointy nails.

"Can you be in love with someone you've never spoken to?" I asked.

"Sure you can," Aunt Virginia said. "I've been in love with the guy on the Old Spice commercial for years." She nudged Lacy, who was curled up beneath the table. "What's that bagel doing in the house?"

"We thought we'd eat her toasted with cream cheese and huckleberry jam for supper," Pa said from his seat on the sofa.

"I do declare, little brother made a funny," Aunt Virginia said. "The Man of Steel is turning into a comedian."

Pa grunted and headed for the back door.

"Are you going to church with us, Pa?" I asked.

He shook his head. "Got work to do."

"Sunday is the day of rest," Aunt Virginia said. "Take a break, little brother."

Pa snorted and went outside.

I looked at Aunt Virginia, who was pressing shiny heart-shaped stickers onto her Metallic Mauve nails. "Were you in love when you were twelve?" I asked.

"I was in love when I was three," Aunt Virginia replied. "Why are you asking all these questions, Maizie? Are you in love?"

"She's in love," Grace called from the living room, where she was playing with her dolls.

"Shush, Grace," I said.

"She's in love with Jonathan Shepherd, who hates girls with red hair and skinny white legs." Grace giggled.

"Is he cute?" Aunt Virginia asked.

"Yes," I said.

"No," Grace said. "He says bad words and burps and picks his nose."

"Nobody's perfect," Aunt Virginia said, blowing on her nails.

I got Grace's halo from the top of the refrigerator and perched it on her head. "His father is a preacher and his mother is beautiful and he lives in a big fancy house over on Candycane Lane." Candycane Lane was the rich people's part of the mountain, where all the city folks settled to get out of the rat race.

"Is he nice?" asked Aunt Virginia.

"How would I know?" I said. "I've never talked to him."

"You're probably just in love with the *idea* of Jonathan Shepherd, not Jonathan Shepherd himself," Aunt Virginia said. "If you were really in love with him, you wouldn't care about his father or his mother or his big fancy house."

"She has Mrs. Shepherd in our Mama Wish Book," said Grace. "She cut it out of the church album."

"Sounds like you're in love with the idea of a mama, too," Aunt Virginia said.

"She wrote two letters to our mama, but

Mama didn't write back," Grace said. "The mailman has the flu."

Aunt Virginia looked at me sideways. "You wrote to your mother? What did you say?"

"Everything," I said.

"Where'd you get the address?"

"From Pa's filing cabinet," I said. "Nobody else has it."

Aunt Virginia lowered her eyes and took a deep breath. "I have a confession to make, darlin'. I've been writing to Ruby for the past four years, telling her all about you girls."

I caught my breath. "What does she say?"

"Nothing. She doesn't answer." Aunt Virginia sighed. "I reckon she wants to be done with the old and get on with the new."

"She might be coming back," Grace said, mounting a Barbie doll astride Lacy's back.

"Don't count your chickens before they're hatched, child," Aunt Virginia said, and we all were quiet for a few minutes.

"Lacy is a raspberry roan," Grace

chanted, bouncing the doll up and down on the dog's back.

"A strawberry roan," I corrected her for the hundredth time.

Grace nodded and the halo bobbed.

"When are you getting that pony?" Aunt Virginia asked. I'd already told her about Donna Texas.

"Sometime in early September," I said. "One of my wishes will be coming true next month."

"If she has enough money," Grace said.

"Oh, I'll have the money, all right," I said with a wink. "I had a good idea this morning." I gazed out the window at Pa, scattering chicken feed on the ground and clucking to the hens.

"What, Maizie?" Grace leaped onto my lap and her halo whacked me in the chin. "What's your good idea?" Grace loved my good ideas almost as much as she loved my stories.

"You know the fertile eggs Harriet lays? The pretty brown ones with the maroon speckles and the red spot inside?"

Grace nodded.

"I found out from Brother Roe that the health-food store sells fertile eggs for almost three dollars a dozen. I'm going to sell Harriet's eggs to Brother Roe's store," I announced.

"Just goes to show that health means wealth," Aunt Virginia said. "Good idea, sugar."

"Brother Roe is your boyfriend, right?" Grace asked Aunt Virginia.

"A *friend*, child. Roe is my friend." Aunt Virginia tapped her nails on the table.

"Do you think that Pa will ever fall in love with anyone?" I asked.

Aunt Virginia shook her head. "If you've been burned once, you're not likely to play with fire again," she said. "Your pa was hurt through and through when your mama left."

I looked out the window again and watched Pa patting Wooly Girl's curly-haired head. "I'm also going to sell Wooly Girl's wool to the sheepskin place the next time she gets sheared," I announced, as if the idea had been brewing for months.

"Not a baaaaad idea," Aunt Virginia bleated.

Pa had made his way out to Mrs. Porkenbean and was rubbing her snout. "Pa is hard as nails on the outside, but on the inside he's milk toast," I said.

"For those times when you can't crack through the steel, remember you can count on me," Aunt Virginia said. "Growing up is the hardest thing you'll ever have to do."

"Does she have to grow up?" Grace asked.

"Pa said that Mama never grew up," I added.

Aunt Virginia just stared at her hands, then at Lacy, then at me. "Let me paint your nails before church, Maizie. Metallic Mauve will go good with that yellow dress of yours."

Grace looked up at me with one patched eye and one blue eye and said, "Jonathan Shepherd hates girls with purple fingernails."

CHAPTER 18

News in a Red Satin Dress

Brother Roe stood up. "I have an announcement to make," he blared. His face was shiny with sweat.

"Not again," I whispered to Becky. "That man must collect announcements."

The church was hot and stuffy, and a mosquito kept buzzing around my ears. It hadn't rained for weeks and the humidity seemed to jump down from the muggy sky and grab you by the throat. What a day for Aunt Virginia to finally attend church.

When we walked in, Gertrude's eyes almost bugged out through her glasses, then she whipped around and began whispering to her bifocaled daughter Gurdy Sue.

"They're gossiping about us," I whispered in Aunt Virginia's ear.

Aunt Virginia swatted it off like a mosquito. "Gossip," she said, "is nothing more than news in a red satin dress."

"Busybodies have nothing better to do than wag their tongues all day long," I complained.

And now it seemed as if every eye in the church was fixed on Aunt Virginia, who hadn't visited the house of the Lord for more than a month of Sundays.

"My news will surprise many of you. . . ." Brother Roe liked to drag his announcements out as long as possible, like Grace licking an ice cream cone.

"My announcement today is that I am engaged to marry . . ." A gasp floated up from the congregation. "Miss Virginia Musser."

"Aunt Virginia! I thought you said he wasn't your boyfriend!" I nudged her bony ribs.

Aunt Virginia smiled straight ahead at the

altar. From the side of her lipsticked mouth, she hissed, "He's not. He's my fiancé."

"You said he was your friend," I accused.

Aunt Virginia smiled. "He'd better be my friend if I'm going to live with him for the rest of my life," she said.

"But you said you weren't in love with Brother Roe." Grace's voice rang out like a choir of angels. Her halo bobbed indignantly.

"I'm not *in love* with him," Aunt Virginia said. "I *love* him. There's a difference."

Jonathan Shepherd turned around and stared.

"Sssshh," I said to Grace and Aunt Virginia.

Sissy Fisher raised her dimpled arms above the old piano and struck the opening chords of "Amazing Grace."

"Here's our song, Maizie," Grace said out loud, as delighted as if Sissy Fisher were some radio disc jockey playing our request. "This is my very favorite church song."

Sissy smiled out at the congregation, her plump pink cheeks bulging with pleasure.

Her stout fingers pounded the piano keys as we launched into the words of the song.

Grace climbed onto the pew behind me as we stood. She turned to watch as the doors swung open and a woman tiptoed in. "Mama!" she whispered. "Maizie, it's our mama."

I could see the woman from the corner of my eye, but I was as scared to turn around as I would have been if the Devil himself had snuck into the sanctuary. "Are you sure, Grace?" I whispered. My heart was pounding harder than the piano keys.

"I'm sure," she said.

I slowly turned my head, which weighed a ton. I looked at the woman, who had long silky hair the color of beets and green-pepper-colored eyes. Our mama had blue eyes. "Grace," I said, "that's not her."

Grace blinked. "Oh," she said.

My head was still heavy, and something screamed inside my soul. Red flashed through the stained glass windows, and I realized that fire sirens were wailing.

"I have an announcement," Brother Roe

bellowed. "There seems to be a fire somewhere up the mountain." He waddled to the
door and peered out.

Brother Roe's face was as red as flames
when he swung around and announced to
the congregation of the Welsh Mountain As-
sembly of the Lord, "The fire appears to be
somewhere in the area of Blue Moon Nursing Home or Jake Musser's trailer."

CHAPTER 19

Up in Smoke

"Why is Gertrude's barn burning?" asked Grace.

"I don't know, Grace. I don't know everything, you know." My eyes stung from the smoke.

Aunt Virginia pushed her damp blonde hair away from her forehead. "Sometimes things like this just happen, sugar." She lifted Grace up to watch the fire trucks.

Mamaw Blue cast a sideways glance at Aunt Virginia. "What woman in her right mind would marry my Roe?" she muttered, fire reflecting in her glasses. Brother Roe had picked her up at Blue Moon and announced his engagement on the way to the fire.

Aunt Virginia ignored Mamaw Blue and snuggled up closer to Brother Roe. I couldn't believe she'd kept all this a secret, and especially from *me*, her Sunday daughter.

Pastor John moseyed over. "It probably started with a discarded match or cigarette," he said. "Happens quite often in dry times like these. If there was straw in there, it would go up in flames like that." He snapped his fingers. Pastor John was assistant fire chief, in addition to preacher and notary public.

Practically the entire congregation, except for Sissy Fisher, had followed the fire engines up the mountain. She would probably go on playing hymns if the world was coming to an end. I could imagine her now, pounding out "The Old Rugged Cross" to the empty pews.

"Where will your roan pony live?" asked Grace.

I sighed. "Don't worry about tomorrow, Grace. Live for the moment." I said it more for myself than for her.

Becky examined her black onyx ring, then

looked at me. "Maybe you could board your pony in a section of our garage, Maizie. You'd have to build a stall."

Aunt Virginia fiddled with an earring. "That would be lots of hard work, sugar."

"Hard work never hurt anybody," I said. "Thank you for the offer, Becky."

"That's what friends are for," Becky said. Her hair was frizzed out around her face, and beads of sweat dotted her nose.

"What are friends for?" asked Brother Roe, unbuttoning his collar. I hoped that Aunt Virginia got rid of that static cling and ring, once they were married.

"To marry," said Aunt Virginia. "Friends are to marry."

I stared at them, trying to picture those two cast in plastic and stuck on top of a fancy wedding cake. They weren't like any couple I'd ever seen in magazines.

"I have an announcement," Brother Roe said, putting his arm around Aunt Virginia.

I rolled my eyes at Becky.

"Mother," said Brother Roe, "this announcement is mostly for you."

Mamaw Blue crossed her arms and looked at him.

"Virginia and I have decided that after we get married next month, we'll move you back into the farmhouse, to live with us. No more Blue Moon." Brother Roe pulled out a gray handkerchief and swabbed at his neck.

"Hallelujah!" hollered Mamaw Blue, waving her arms above her head. "No more calf-poop days."

Aunt Virginia and Brother Roe exchanged a look, while Grace hopped up and down and clapped her hands.

"Hooray!" she shouted. "Now we can dig for money anytime we want!"

"Sugar," said Aunt Virginia, picking Grace up by the waist and twirling her in a circle, "you'll have such a collection of coffee cans that you'd best open yourself a grocery store."

"Hooray!" hollered Grace again as Gertrude lumbered across the yard, huffing and puffing.

"Too bad, Maizie," she said, thumping my back. "Seems like you hit on all the hard

times. Just like when that mama of yours ran
out. . . ."

"Gertrude," I said. "Meet my Aunt Virginia."

Gertrude eyed her up and down. "Pleased
to see you in church this morning," she said.
"We don't turn anybody away, not even—"

I cut her off cold. "Gertrude, do you think
the barn can be saved, at least part of it?"

"Well, Maizie, that's not up to me to say."
Gertrude took off her glasses and rubbed her
full-moon face. "You'd have to talk to an expert, and one thing I'm not is an expert. At
least not in building matters. Now, human
nature is another thing entirely. Harvey used
to say that I could read people like books. For
example, Pastor John is the Bible, your Aunt
Virginia here is a dimestore novel, Brother
Roe is a fact book, Grace is a comic, and you,
Maizie, are a mystery. Now that mama of
yours would have been some of that cheap ro-
mance trash. Harvey used to say . . ."

I didn't care what Harvey used to say. In
fact, I didn't really care what Gertrude had
to say, especially if all she wanted to do was

cut my mama into bits with that razor-sharp tongue of hers. Every time she sliced my mama, I bled a little bit, too.

"I'll get Pa to take a look at the barn," I said, changing Gertrude's subject.

"I already did." Pa stood behind me.

"Pa! What are you doing here?"

He picked some pieces of straw from his hair and lowered his eyes. "Cleaning the barn," he said. "Wanted to surprise you for your birthday."

"You were here before the fire started, Mr. Musser?" Pastor John stuck his hands in his suit pockets.

"Yep." Pa nodded. "I was here when the fire started." He scuffed his workboot in the grass. "Started in the back stall."

"You weren't smoking, by any chance?" Pastor John narrowed his gray eyes and coughed.

Pa nodded.

"And what were you doing smoking, Jake Musser?" It was Doc Jeffries. "I warned you that you were ruining your health." His face was stern beneath his white hair.

Pa just hung his head and rubbed his temples.

Pastor John's eyes burned into Pa's soul. "You didn't happen to throw down a cigarette, by any chance?" he asked.

Pa nodded slowly, as if a string pulled his head up and down.

"Oh, Pa," I said.

Pa's eyes watered. "I'm sorry, Maizie. I know how bad you want that strawberry roan."

I put my arm around Pa's shoulder. I was getting to be just about as tall as my pa. "It's okay, Pa," I said. "I will get that pony or my name's not Maizie Musser." But in my mind, I was running against the wind, just like the strawberry roan on the cover of my Wish Book.

Pa's shoulder twitched beneath my touch. He took a deep breath, and I felt the gaunt bones beneath his torn workshirt. "Maizie," he said, "I have a birthday gift for you. No more smoking." He took the pack of cigarettes from his pocket and tossed them into the smoldering pile of what used to be Gertrude's barn.

I smooched Pa's stubbly cheek, something I hadn't done for years. "Thank you, Pa," I said. "That sure is a wish come true."

Grace tugged on Pa's arm. "You shouldn't have been working on a Sunday, Pa." Her sparkly gown was now a dingy brown.

I looked at Pa. "Shouldn't-have-beens don't count, Grace," I said.

Aunt Virginia stroked Grace's hair, which was blacker than ever beneath the white halo. "You missed the chance to see Grace be an angel," she said to Pa.

Pa shrugged. "Won't be the first chance I've missed in my life," he said.

And then we all fell silent as we stood together and watched Gertrude's old barn and Pa's bad habit go up in smoke.

Little did I know that within the week one of my wishes, too, would go up in smoke.

CHAPTER 20

A Rainbow Fable

I yanked open the mailbox. There was the electric bill, an ad from Charlie's Cut Rate, and a letter from Mr. Flynn. I decided to save the best for last, which was the glossy brochure stuffed full of all the latest sales down at Charlie's.

"Might as well get the worst over with," I muttered, and slowly peeled open the electric bill. "Overdue balance: $105.29," it read. That wasn't so bad; I'd seen worse, much worse. I'd give Pa some money to help out again. After all, he kept a roof over my head and food on the table.

I ripped open the white envelope from Mr.

Flynn. There was a piece of lined yellow notebook paper inside. *Maizie, I've had a change of heart. A brown and pink pony will look dandy in that spiffy red barn. Flynn.*

My heart galloped. "Donna Texas, here you come to the Welsh Mountain!" I shouted. "Maizie Musser is ready for you . . . finally!" My voice echoed across the mountain.

Humming, I opened the ad from Charlie's Cut Rate and something fell out. It was a postcard, slick and glistening with a brilliant rainbow arching across the front. When I turned it over, goose bumps prickled across my arms. It was from Mama.

Maizie/Grace,

Hi! Good news! You have a baby brother. He was born on July 24, his name is Donald Junior, and he's the cutest little pumpkin you'd ever want to see! Don and I were married last year and honeymooned in Bermuda. I'm owner of a company called Ruby Cosmetics, and of course Don is still selling Rainbows.

Last month, he sold fifteen Rainbows and I gave myself the top Ruby award! It's a piece of cake to sell makeup and vacuum cleaners here in Pittsburgh because the people like to make themselves and their homes beautiful. Different from the hillbillies on that molehill you call a mountain. Till we meet again . . . Your Mother.

The postcard smelled like perfume. I pressed it to my nose and next to my heart. Then I threw myself on the ground and bawled like a baby for the first time since The Leaving.

Mama was never coming back. She wasn't coming back to say good-bye or to say hello or to say I love you. She was never coming back and that's all there was to it.

I keened and wailed and screamed at the mama who would never hear my cries or be there when I needed her. "I hate you, Mama. I hate you," I sobbed, pounding on the ground. "I love you, Mama." I figured it didn't really matter what I said because she'd never hear me. She'd never hear anything I ever said.

Then, after I'd cried out my eyes and my heart and my soul, I stuck the postcard in my pocket, wiped my nose, and went inside to make supper.

Later, as I tucked Grace in for the night, I said, "We got a postcard from Mama." I still smelled the perfume.

Grace's eyes widened. "Is she coming back?"

I picked up Sed and cradled him in my arms. "No," I said.

"Why not?"

"She doesn't belong here on the mountain. It's not her home anymore." I plucked at Sed's fur.

"Is she still our mother?" Grace was so small, all curled up on our bed and hugging her pillow.

"Yes, Grace," I said. "She'll always be our mother."

"Did she say why she left?" Grace asked.

"She just had to, that's all." I placed Sed next to Grace.

"Did she send a picture?"

"No," I said, staring at the tiny scar above Grace's left eye. "We'll just have to see her inside ourselves. That's better, anyway, because we can make her anything we want her to be."

"I'm going to make her pretty," Grace said, yawning. "What do you think the Rainbow man looks like?"

"Bald," I said.

Grace giggled. "Do you think we'll ever have a baby brother like the ones in our Wish Book?"

I thought a moment. "Nah," I said. "Mama said we'd be a hard act to follow."

Grace nodded solemnly. "What else did she say?"

"Oh, she said that she loves us and that we're in her heart forever. She said that when she carried us in her belly, below her heart, we each reached up and ripped off a tiny chunk of her heart. And now, no matter where we are or where Mama is, we're always together." It was a lie (the third one of the summer), but I reckoned that God would understand. After all, He was the one who gave mamas the instinct to protect their young. And I was the closest thing to a mama that Grace would have. Ever.

"Did Mama ask what I look like?"

"Of course she did. She hasn't seen you since you were a bald-headed baby, you know."

"Bald like the Rainbow man?" Grace asked.

"Just like that," I said.

"What are you going to tell her about me when you write again, Maizie?"

"That you're beautiful like her and ornery like Pa and that she'd be mighty proud," I said.

"Are you going to tell her that I brush my own hair? And that I eat squash now?"

"I'm going to tell her everything," I said. "She said to tell you that you'd better eat lots of meat and vegetables. She wants you to grow up healthy."

Grace smiled. "I guess she really does love us."

"I guess she does," I said. "Mamas always love their babies."

"What about Mamaw Blue and Brother Roe?" Grace asked. "She says that she can't stand him and that he's too big for his britches and that he's got a swelled head."

"That's all just talk," I said, sorry that I'd told her all that. "When it comes right down to it, Mamaw Blue would give her right arm for her son. She loves him; it's just that she doesn't always like him."

"Like you and me?" Grace asked.

"Like you and me," I said, reaching out and tousling her hair.

"Tell me a story before bed," Grace said. "Tell me a Rainbow Fable."

"I already did," I said, and turned off the light.

I walked slowly down the hall to the bathroom and got the scissors that we used to cut out pictures for our Wish Books. Looking into the cracked mirror above the sink, I started to snip at my hair. I cut off all the split ends, and then I trimmed my bangs, and then I took a couple of inches off the sides. There was a pile of my hair in the sink . . . strawberry-blonde hair, just like Mama's.

When I looked in the mirror, I saw a new Maizie, one who was older and wiser and more worldly-looking than ever before. The Maizie I'd been for almost thirteen years was left behind, like the hair in the sink, and the new one was looking me right in the eyes.

CHAPTER 21

Skimming Stones and Spitting Nails

It was half past dark on a Saturday night, the day before my birthday, and Becky and I were sitting by the Deep Hole, skimming stones and watching the Jesus bugs walk on water.

The Deep Hole is an old swimming hole sunk into the middle of the mountain, and everybody says it's bottomless. I don't know if that's true, but I do know that I've never touched the bottom. Pa says that if anybody ever tried, they'd end up in China.

"Can you believe that the summer's almost over?" Becky asked, dangling her feet in the murky green water.

I shook my head and dabbled some water on my legs. "It flew by like a scared cat," I said.

Becky looked at me. "Why'd you cut your hair, Maizie?" she asked. "I liked it long."

"Sometimes you're just ready for a change," I said. "A beginning, like when the caterpillar sheds its cocoon and becomes a butterfly."

Becky smiled. "You do have a way with words, Maizie. You should write a book."

"Someday," I said, skimming a smooth white pebble across the water. It skipped three times and then plopped down to China.

"You know the funny thing about Jesus bugs?" Becky asked. Without waiting for me to answer, she said, "The funny thing is, they can skim and skate across the water in the blink of an eye, but they don't know how to swim. If a big wave ever crashed over them, they'd drown."

I nodded and watched the little critters skate on their spindly legs. It's hard to imagine that those skinny bugs are spunky enough to walk on water even though they can't swim. I guess that's how life is; you just have to be like the Jesus bugs and be plucky enough to face it with some grit and a lot of guts and hope that a big wave never comes.

"Are you daydreaming again, Maizie?" Becky asked, sloshing some of that stagnant water over my head. "Wake up."

"I'm awake," I said. "I'm not a dreamer anymore."

When Becky looked at me, the moonlight glowed silvery gold in her glasses. "I know that tone of voice, Maizie Musser. You're thinking about your mama again."

"I reckon I always will," I said quietly.

Becky threw a stone, hard, against the other bank of the Deep Hole. "How do you stand it?" she asked. "Her off having a good old time in Pittsburgh and you slaving away on the Welsh Mountain?"

I shrugged. "Mama was wrong to leave," I said. "But if you love somebody, you forgive them."

"How?" Becky asked. "I have a hard time forgiving Daddy when he forgets to bring something home for me. How can you forgive a mother who forgets to bring *herself* home?"

"Becky," I said, "I'm going to tell you something that nobody else in this world knows. Remember how I found that locket in Mama's sock drawer after she left?"

Becky nodded.

"Well, the locket wasn't the only thing I found. Tucked way back in the corner of the drawer, beneath an old holey pair of socks, I found a Bible. A tiny, pocket-size Bible with a red leather cover and a zipper around the edges. And when I opened that zipper, I found a page that said, 'To Ruby, our precious jewel, on your thirteenth birthday. May you always find happiness. Love, Mom and Pop.' "

I swallowed hard. "And I also found a passage that Mama must have circled. It was all about love, how it's patient and kind and trusting. How it's not jealous or rude or selfish. How it doesn't remember wrongs."

Becky gazed into the Deep Hole. "Reading it and doing it are two different things," she said. "How can you love somebody who doesn't love you back?"

"Unconditional love," I said. "Like when your dog still loves you even though you forget to feed him. It's just love, plain and simple, with no strings attached."

Becky laughed. "Too bad you don't have strings attached to your mama so you could pull her back home."

"I wouldn't even if I could, Becky. Remember that poster in school that said if you love something, you set it free?"

Becky nodded.

"Well, I've finally set Mama free. I've finally let go."

"She just wanted to escape, Maizie, and leave you with all the burdens."

I sighed. "Everybody wants to escape something. Pa wanted to escape from reality, so he drank. Mama wanted to escape from kids and now she has another one. Escaping doesn't work."

Becky thought for a moment. "So what did you do with the Bible?" she asked.

I laughed, suddenly embarrassed. "Stuck

it beneath Pa's mattress," I said. "I was hoping that by keeping something of Mama's close to Pa's dreams, it would bring her back. Like magic." I looked at Becky. "Remember how I used to think that if I ever got that locket open, it would be magic?"

Becky chuckled and nodded.

"Well, I learned that the only magic in this world comes from within. You have to make your own magic and make your own wishes come true. And some of those wishes, the ones that can never come true, just have to fly away."

"So," Becky said, staring at the water, "is the Bible still under your pa's mattress?"

"No," I said. "The day I got Mama's postcard, I took it out and hid it with my Wish Books. I'm going to save it for when I have kids someday. You know, pass it down just like your grandmother taught your mother to play Hoss and she taught it to you. On down the line."

"So what did your mother ever give to you, Maizie Musser?"

I pondered. "Life," I said.

"You're just too nice," Becky said. "Don't you ever get real mad?"

"Sometimes I'm so mad I could spit nails," I said.

Becky skipped a stone across the Deep Hole. "So do it," she said. "Spit nails."

I counted the skips: one, two, three, four. Then I looked up at the man in the moon, the same moon that shines on Pittsburgh. I imagined Mama lounging on the patio of her fancy apartment in the light of that moon, and I suddenly got very angry.

It was then that I knew what I had to do.

CHAPTER 22

The Slamming of a Door

Dear Mama,

Thirteen years ago tomorrow, you gave birth to me and I caused you much pain. Now you're the one causing me to hurt.

I'm hurt and I'm sad and I'm mad, and I guess I always will be. All because you went searching for a pot of gold somewhere over the Rainbow. I sometimes wonder if you couldn't have waited until Grace and I were grown-up and then went searching, instead of being so all-fired impatient. Patience is a virtue, you know.

When I was younger, I used to look at your old high school graduation picture and pretend that I was the twinkle in your left eye and Grace was the one in your right eye. But I was blind, Mama, because I couldn't see that the only light in your life is yourself.

What did you run away from, Mama? You know, you can travel all over this world and still stay where you are because you're always going to wake up with yourself.

The one thing in this world that I still wish for is your love. But, as you told Pa when you left, you can't give away what you don't have. So I reckon I'll just stop wishing, after this one last wish.

I wish you happiness, Mama. I wish you happiness and peace and love. I wish all your wishes come true someday.

As for me, I'll be fine. I'm tougher than I look. When you first left, I used to make lists of girls who grew up without mamas and who turned out okay. Snow

White and Cinderella lived happily ever after, and so will Maizie Musser.

I'll always love you and I'll always remember you, even when it hurts. And I'll be fine.

And now I must get to bed and get some sleep, Mama, because tomorrow's going to be a big day.

Love, Maizie.

On the bottom of the letter, I drew a picture of Mama as I remembered her, with long wavy hair and catlike eyes. It was the first time I'd ever been able to draw Mama.

I folded the letter in half and put it in the fancy apricot-colored stationery box, where I'd been hiding Mama's postcard. On the lid I wrote MAMA'S MEMORY BOX.

I went outside and picked a sprig of lilac from the edge of the garden and put that in Mama's Memory Box. Smells can bring a person back to you in the whiff of a moment.

I took the heart locket from around my neck and opened it. Mama, Pa, Grace, and the Maizie of five years ago smiled up at me. I smiled at the picture and then pried it from the locket. Behind the photo was another one: the Rainbow man leaning against our back door when it was shiny and new and undented by Wooly Girl's hooves.

I glared at the Rainbow man for a moment and then studied the other picture, which had ripped when I pulled it from the locket. "That figures," I said to the smirking Rainbow man. "You tore our family apart five years ago, and now you're doing it again."

Then I tore the Rainbow man into a zillion pieces and tossed them in the trash can.

I carefully laid the locket and our family picture in Mama's Memory Box.

I tiptoed into our bedroom and dug out the Wish Books, the little red Bible, and the black velvet bow Gertrude had given to me. I carried my bounty back out to the kitchen and plopped it down on the oilcloth.

Opening the Mama Wish Book, I slowly pulled the first page from the spiral-bound notebook. Mama's graduation picture, hemmed in with squiggly cursive writing, went into the Memory Box.

The Mama Wish Book, with all its glossy and glamorous mothers, whizzed into the trash can to join the Rainbow man.

A tiny snip of my hair, so like Mama's, for the Memory Box. Then I arranged the black velvet bow on the strawberry-blonde strands and admired the sequins glittering in the glow of the kerosene lantern.

I tucked the red leather Bible in a cardboard corner, and then I closed the lid to Mama's Memory Box.

"I wonder if I'll ever get to see the ocean?" I said to myself as I studied the pictures of seashells floating around the edges of the stationery box. "That would be nice, but if it never happens, I won't wish for it because I'm happy right here where I am."

I snuck into the bedroom again and stashed Mama's Memory Box in the back right corner of the closet I share with Grace. Then I lugged the rest of the Wish Books—

Baby Brother, Mamaw and Papaw, and Horse—over to the trash can and dumped them in.

They fell with a final thud . . . like the slamming of a door.